WALKING

NOVELS BY TOBY OLSON

The Life of Jesus
Seaview
The Woman Who Escaped From Shame
Utah
Dorit in Lesbos
At Sea
Write Letter to Billy
The Blond Box
The Bitter Half
Tampico

WALKING

a love story

by

TOBY OLSON

OCCIDENTAL SQUARE BOOKS

SEATTLE 2020

Editorial and design copyright Chatwin Books

Editorial assistance by Megan Gray

Interior design by Vladimir Verano

Cover photograph by Rex Wilder

Cover design by Vladimir Verano

paperback: ISBN 978-1-63398-091-4

ebook: ISBN 978-1-63398-109-6

Chatwin Books
www.chatwinbooks.com

For Lois.

Under your wing this book was written.

With Love,

Toby

Excess of grief for the dead
is madness; for it is an injury
to the living, and the dead
know it not.

Xenophon

TABLE OF CONTENTS

CHAPTER 1

APHRODITE,

4:30 am

My mother is dead now, as is my father, at least he has been declared dead. Once I left Wisconsin I never saw him again. Bless his wicked soul, he left me all the money I'll ever need, though I don't need much. Most of the time I sleep in the women's shelter at the peninsula's end, or I stay with men, or on occasion I rent a room for a few months.

I walked here from Wisconsin a good many years ago. Well, not all the way. I rode the occasional bus, walking up and down the aisles, getting nowhere, while the bus took me somewhere. It was an awkward enterprise at best and now seems somewhat silly. I'm sure the bus passengers saw it as such. And so I'd climb down after only a few miles and would resume my walking.

It all started, or at least I began to notice it, when I was in the fifth grade, and it continued until I walked away from it after graduating from high school. My mother had taken to her bed at that earlier time, and she was never to rise out of it again. They said she had Chronic Fatigue Syndrome and believed the cause to be depression. That seems likely to me now, looking back. She was exhausted, weak in body, worn out, and her care was left to the nurses my father hired, not to my father, nor to me. Quickly, she became no more than a shade in our household, and as she did so I became something other than the child I was then.

How obvious. It was of course my father.

My father was a dealer, or better a purveyor of rare, often ancient dolls, ones that he bought, then sold at a significant profit. Some needed repair, and that took place in his "office" down in the basement. Others he posed in numerous places throughout the house, bald heads and naked bodies, some clothed in garments he had sewn up and ironed so that they fell as if new from wood and porcelain shoulders. Little hats as well and tiny black patent leather shoes.

They were not there for touching.

He had a small office in town, but that was seldom used. He worked in the house, down in the basement, where he kept his anxiety-ridden capuchin monkey in a cage, or at time in the kitchen, where he would cover the table with his wares. He seemed always to be wherever I was.

I'd come home from school, and he would sit me down in the living room and ask me about my day, the teachers, the studies, the sports. He had a small rubber figure, a child's head extracted from a mold he'd fashioned in the basement. Soft rubber. And he would squeeze it in his chubby hand when he spoke to me. He was a fat man with a round face and a thin mustache, always carefully trimmed and in later years dyed black with a small fragile brush. He was not bald then, but was getting there, and he combed his hair forward to cover his broad forehead. His dress was always casual, khaki pants, white socks and tennis shoes and a blue chambray work shirt open at the collar, where his graying chest hair curled out. A thin belt, his corpulent stomach hanging over to hide a portion of it. His name was Rodney Appell. He'd be sixty years old now. Some kids called me apple at school.

And he would at times take my picture with his old Pentax camera. When I was young, he might have to speak, in his gentle way, asking me to stop fidgeting, to sit still. Then, on my birthday, every year until I left, he would take my picture in profile. To preserve me, he'd say with a smile. I didn't know where he kept these pictures, if he kept them at all.

And he would look at me. Never at my body, but always directly in my eyes, as he was squeezing his little rubber doll's head. And I can remember no expression in his face or his smiles or his sympathetic frowns, nothing in any way provocative or, what shall I call it, sexual? It was his eyes only. No squinting or focusing, just gazing into my own. It was hard to look away, for when I did, then looked back again, his gaze was as before, steady, casual and intense at the same time. His pupils floated amongst chips of blue ice, but with a kind of shadowy intention deep within them, something dirty and forbidden. I can try to name it now, but then I could only feel it, a kind of penetration.

And when his questions and comments and his feigned sympathy and engagement seemed at an ending, or more often when I saw a pause that I could turn into an ending, I would excuse myself—the bathroom, a snack, a visit with my mother in her bedroom—and would walk out of the oppression of that space into the relative freedom of another, the kitchen, the dining room, even the basement, where he pursued his hobby, tiny theater dioramas with little curtains that opened on groups of dancing children in shorts and tutus, their garments fashioned from cuttings of the clothing my mother no longer wore, being bedridden. And his monkey, gripping the bars of its cage and glaring at me. And then, of course, he would follow me, sit me down again, then penetrate me with those eyes of his, and I would once again have to rise and walk away into other rooms and free spaces. Again and again.

He seldom left me, though there was respite now and then, when he was working, in the basement or was visiting my mother in her bed. I could hear his soft, gentle voice then, but not the words, the creak of the bed as he sat down beside her wasted body, occasionally groaning. And at times I found myself on my feet, even though he was not pursuing me. I'd walk through the rooms and out on the covered porch that ran around three sides of the house, then down the wooden steps to pace the sidewalks, around the block, and sometimes into the center of the town, passing shops, gas stations, town hall, and even walking the streets that took me to the shore of Lake Winnebago, a mile or so away.

And I have been walking ever since.

Once, I crept to the bathroom door. I knew my father was in there. I had been studying at the kitchen table, my legs hanging down from the high stool I sat on, when I heard a kind of rattling coming from the little bathroom that connected to the kitchen. A few soft steps and I was there, my ear pressed against the hollow door.

My father was making the most unearthly sounds. A tortured groaning, a cackling laughter and a wheezing, and under it all a kind of rhythm, intensifying, then receding. And it was then that I recognized the faint clattering sound that had drawn me there. It was my father's charm bracelet. Every year of my life my father documented with a little gold silhouette of my head. And there, now, these small gold figures were jumping and rattling against each other. I could imagine them hanging from their chain at his thin, pale wrist.

What was he doing in there? Brushing his teeth?

I was no more than a child then, innocent and furtive.

Later, under hand towels in the cabinet beside the toilet, I found my fifth grade class photo. My school was a small private one, no more than fifteen students in each grade-school class, and someone, my father I assumed, who else could it be?, had drawn a neat black circle around my head, there where I sat at the end of the second row, smiling. I put the picture back where I had found it.

Isn't that cute, I thought.

The guy I left this morning was a four-nighter. I met him when I was walking back one evening. He was jogging. He needed it. He pulled up and walked beside me, breathing heavily, and once we'd passed a few words, I ended up at his place, some dinner, and then to bed.

He was deep in sleep, just a wheezing lump beneath the blanket, when I crept from his bed. It was four o'clock and still dark, and after I'd washed and powdered my thighs, I stepped into the darkness at peninsula's end. Now I am walking.

Sand dunes rise silvery in first light on my left. There are few cars this early, and I walk on cement and ribbons of blacktop repair in the bike path curving along the two lane highway, heading for the magical beach town, many miles away.

A foggy day, but that will burn off quickly as the sun heats up. A light breeze pushes my backpack, and I quicken my pace. There is this one main artery. It bleeds out at the place I'm heading for, the peninsula's beginning, where there is passage to the rest of America. Miles to go. My feet tell me I have logged only a few, three or four. It must be five-thirty. The traffic has picked up a little. Some who have seen me in this daily passage wave.

The dunes flatten and recede. Gulls and terns rise up from the beach off in the distance. I can see it and the sea too when there's a break in the pines and scrub oak. It is somewhat beautiful but in no way inviting. It's very difficult to walk in sand, and I avoid it. All my life I have been walking, sometimes getting places, but not often. I feel him again, and as I'm on an incline now, I push harder. The town will be a place of brief respite when I get there. I have food in my pack and will pick up a bottle of water. I might even walk about for a while, watching the tourists and locals in the town and at the amusement park between it and the beach and sea before heading back. There are numerous Mexican vendors there, some in white coats looking much like Good Humor men, selling ices and ice cream, and at times the Tall Ships come from their docks in the city and round the mountain where the peninsula begins. Massive, even at a distance, and under full sail, they make their way slowly, dark silhouetted figures backed by the setting sun. Their black sheets are taut, holding a windblown from the mouth of time that threatens to swallow us all, the sea still and empty behind them as they fade away. Shadows cast from amusement park rides pattern the sand both day and night. I'm often there after dark and have seen all this.

The sun is moving up now. Sparrows and chickadees chirp softly in the pines and oaks. A light breeze rustles leaves. I hear the faint sound of coyotes howling deep in the woods. And boldly from the scrub ahead a red fox emerges, pauses, then crosses the highway. Magisterial. Her beautiful raw nature. All this...And a rainbow would be fun, though that's impossible outside my mind. It must be close to 7:00. The sun seems that high.

Time for a little counting. Each step, up to five-hundred, then back again to zero. Something to do. Like humming. I am not bored, nor anxious, nor do I have hopes of getting somewhere. I am just moving. Away, I guess. But for sex and sleeping.

CHAPTER 2

NED HOBBY

As he passed the trash can sitting in front of the closed bodega, he threw the newspaper into it. He was walking home from the gallery, angry and disgusted. The paper held the most recent review of his installation, and it, like all the others, addressed his work as stellar: "Hobby has created something never seen before … An artist to be reckoned with … Do not miss this painful exercise. It pushes art to its limits."

The work in question occupied a large space in the gallery, and as Ned mingled anonymously in the crowd peering through the bars, listening to their whispers and inane comments, it struck him, as it had since the show opened, how uninteresting his art had become.

The critics, the viewers, the obviously kind words of his friends and fellow artists; it was all bullshit. Maybe he was finished or at least needed a break.

Beyond the prison bars that ran across the room, separating the viewers from the installation, stood a row of female manikins. Their postures were identical, copied from a movement in an old ballet Ned had seen years ago and had forgotten the name of it or the story it told. He had dressed them in tutus and short white wigs, and each had a hand on the shoulder of the one in front of her. They were a still parade, and in their provocative garments and naked torsos appeared as little dancing girls, flat-chested and intense, and very still. A broken umbrella, a pile of dirty linen, a sandbox in which rested a scatter of small naked doll figures, and, at one end of the work, a cage in which a fat middle aged man, balding, half naked under his ratty robe, gazed out at the observers with a sour look upon his pitted face. Occasionally, he would move around in his cramped space or sit on the chair that was provided, his head hanging down between his knees. He wore a large heavy bracelet dangling from his thin wrist, and it clattered loudly when he lifted his hand to his brow.

And that was it. Provocative? No way, Ned thought, as he paused for the light at twenty-fourth and eighth, then proceeded to cross and walked south on the avenue. It was all uninteresting, even boring. He needed a drink, but didn't stop at his neighborhood bar. He walked on home. He'd have one there, alone, and without the prospect of any satisfaction. Then he couldn't open the door.

It was the mail the postman had shoved through the slot. A thicket of bills, checks, and professional letters. And once he'd squeezed into his spacious apartment, he carried it all to the kitchen table, not for reading, but for a few minutes of sorting. But first came three fingers of Maker's Mark, ice and spring water in a tall class. There was a letter from his photographer, no doubt a bill. Since his installations couldn't be sold, he had the photographer take a broad range of shots of the works after the gallery closed. The cost of such photography was high, but his dealer was able to sell the photographs for a good deal of money. They were offered in limited editions, the negatives destroyed; at least that was the angle. Ned kept all of them in a safety deposit box at his bank.

Five letters from his agent, probably reviews. He didn't open them. There was one there from his mother, a few from friends and well-wishers, and a half dozen bills: rent, utilities, medical. He'd been suffering of late from pains in his feet. He was diabetic and not very good with his meds and was told the foot problems were typical, peripheral neuropathy. He went for massages, feet and legs, and while that felt very good, it wasn't much help with the problem. And he was a walker, one who searched out objects and scenes in the city, looking for ideas for the next works. His feet pissed him off, and he often swore at them in private.

He sat in front of the television for a while, a fresh drink in hand, thinking about his feet and his art. Then he went into the bathroom and washed up, and while he was brushing his teeth and wondering what to do next, just anything that would take his mind away from whatever it was that was bothering him, he decided he'd give his recent girlfriend Natasha a call. Natasha was an over the hill model from Russia, one whose work was now limited to hand jobs. She had beautiful hands, long, sinewy fingers that in their probing seemed very well educated. Busy with his recent show, he hadn't spoken to her in a while.

"What do you want it, big bastard?" This spoken in her rooskie accent.

"Whoa," he said. "Is there a problem?"

"You haven't called up on me in two weeks! That is the problem."

"Well, the show you know. I've been very busy."

"Busy, my big ass! Well, *I'm* busy. It is now over, shitty face!"

Shitty face?

"Wait, wait! We're going steady."

"Going steady? Going steady? You are fifty-three old years, silly ass. What? Were you going to give it me your pin school letteret sweater?"

"Well, I..."

But she had hung up.

Then the phone rang, his mother, angry Edna Hobby, calling from Florida.

"Did you get my letter?"

"Yes, it's right here."

"Well, what do you think?"

"I don't know. I haven't opened it yet."

"Why not? It's a letter from your mother."

"I just got home."

"Well?"

"What?"

"Well, open the damned thing! Right now!"

"Okay! Okay!"

The letter was full of chatty talk about parties, early bird dinners, and card games—canasta, he thought— at pool side. Then, at the end, came the bombshell. She was getting married. He picked up the phone again.

"Are you serious! Are you sure about this? Who is this guy?"

"This guy, as you call him, is rich. He has a winter place here. He lives up north, in Massachusetts. And it's hot as hell down here. I'm sick of it!"

"How old is he?" She was seventy-three.

"A little younger than I."

" But..."

"Rich! I said. And he's good looking, and the sex is okay."

"Mother!"

"Oh, grow up!" she said. "I want you to give me away."

"What do you mean?"

"At the wedding, for crying out loud! I want you to give your mother away!"

Would that he could.

"Where? When?"

"A little beach town on the coast. Next week."

"Next week! But my show, mother. It's up and running." He was hedging. The show would close in two days.

"Your mother is getting married! Don't you understand?"

"Yes... But... Well..."

"Think about it," she said.

"Okay, okay. I'll call you back."

"No!" she said. "Right now!"

"Okay," he said.

He put the phone down and went back in the kitchen to get another drink, a little awkward now on his feet. Holy mackerel, he thought, this is crazy. How long has she know this guy? The whiskey was sloshing in his glass, some dribbling onto the carpet. I won't do it, he thought. I don't *need* to do it. Then he picked up the phone again.

"Okay," he said. "What's the place called? What day? What time?"

Ned was an only child, and he loved his mother. A little too much in fact, for he didn't really like her. She'd been a trained surgical nurse, now retired, and she'd cared for him as a child with a certain clinical detachment. He'd been a mama's boy growing up, and even at fifty-three, he knew he was still that. Time spent with her was always fraught with childishness on his part, and it seemed to him she enjoyed that, arguing and correcting him at every turn. And now this stupid marriage, and only a year after his father's death. He'd been felled by cancer, and Ned had watched as his mother had wept uncontrollably at the funeral. He and a few others had carried her screaming from the church. And now, much too quickly, she'd put his father behind her. Would she do the same if he were to die?

Good Lord, what nonsense!

He woke in the morning with a throbbing head, the half empty whiskey bottle sitting on his bedside locker. He'd learned that term when he was in the Navy, having joined up right out of high school to get away from his mother. He'd been in for just four years, all of it stateside, working as a hospital corpsman, what other sailors derisively called a pecker checker. He'd avoided going home on leave. He'd seen his mother from time to time, when she'd visited him in the city, but since he didn't get along with his father, he'd never gone back to Florida, but for a few days for his father's funeral.

Immediately after his discharge, he'd enrolled at the Fashion Institute, majoring in visual presentation and exhibition design, and it was that study that got him a job at Macy's designing their window displays. It was fussing with those windows, dressing, posing and creating elegant and hip environments for numerous plastic figures that got him to consider installation art as a way to get somewhere. Money, he'd thought, and fame, and before he knew it he had both and was for a while happy.

His success had been immediate. Great reviews and crowds and many friends and admirers in the art community. Even a little healthy jealousy. His first piece had been filled with dark business and manikins. Naked dolls and other plastic figures had become a staple in his work, a kind of trademark. He quickly found that all he had to do, as with those Macy window displays, was shift the focus and placement and add a few provocative tableaus in order to get both the critics and the audience to exude an over abundance of praise. And this praise, he'd now begun to see, was the thing that urged him on, piece after piece, and not any sense of the quality of his art, if art is what it was.

Maybe it wasn't.

After he'd showered and dressed and eaten some breakfast, cold cereal with pitted prunes on top, he walked out into the New York summer air, looking for ideas that didn't come, though he kept on walking, up Eighth Avenue, then over to Seventh, then all the way north to Central Park, where he found a bench near a path among trees. He didn't know what kind of trees, and he didn't really care. He just sat there, listening to the birds he couldn't name and the passing walkers, thinking.

Maybe he was burned out. Maybe he needed a little break from his art and this city. Maybe, after the wedding, he should stay on awhile, a little sun-bathing, time spent in bars. Women? So he bought plane tickets with an open return and made hotel reservations.

CHAPTER 3

HUMPHREY EDGEMONT BOGARDUS

THE EDGE PASSED RITTENHOUSE SQUARE, YOUNG lovers on benches, exhausted in the humidity, lazy dogs lying under trees, panting in the grass, a sweating juggler, only three balls in the air and no audience, and an Asian student from the Curtis Institute of Music, sawing away on her violin. The streets were almost empty. He passed shops that were still open, people seen through plate glass, casual shoppers, there not for shopping, but for the moments of relief offered by air conditioning. Good Lord, it was hot. Just six long blocks to go, but it felt like miles. A long way from Paris, or Texas for that matter.

He was heading for Jack's Comfort Inn on Juniper Street, the gay club he played in most weekends, doing standards at the piano bar. It was getting dark now, approaching 8:00, but the city's heat was still oppressive, pedestrians staggering down the street or collapsed in shaded doorways as he passed by. He was walking slowly, shirt stuck to his back with sweat. He'd been chewing a half stick of sugarless gum, but he tossed it into a trash can in front of some bodega. Like so much else, it had turned sour in his mouth. God, I'd love to get away from all this, he thought.

He'd lived in Philadelphia for fifteen years, playing in various venues, most of them gay, many on trips to milder places: Provincetown, Key West in winter, and occasionally on cruise ships that plied the waters among islands in the Caribbean. He was a good looking dude, forty-two years old, tall and fit, aquiline nose and focused blue eyes, dark hair with a touch of grey at the temples, all the rest of that business. Distinguished. The rich quality of his casual summer attire, tan raw-silk pants and a darker brushed cotton shirt, his fine British loafers, was made possible by his other career. On the side and often in the middle, he was a drug dealer: cocaine, marijuana, and ecstasy, exclusively for the wealthy. He hobnobbed a little, yet kept a comfortable distance. There'd be someone later with the goods at Jack's.

He was born as the youngest child on the outskirts of Corpus Christi, Texas. His father was a ranch hand, and his mother had all she could handle in the raising of her six children, all of them boys. She had named him Humphrey because of their last name,

Bogardus. It was a kind of joke for her. She hadn't wanted another, but there he was, and she might as well have some fun. Edgemont came from the father of an old uncle, and thus his nicknames: Humph, Bo, and of course Edge. He became *The Edge* in High School, where he was a star running back on the football team. He provided the edge needed to win every game in his junior and senior years.

Corpus, as was the case with many in Texas, was a football town, the stands always packed with fans and at times college agents, and he received offers from more than a dozen universities. He decided on Temple, much to his father's chagrin. Temple was no football power, but it had a fine music department, and since he had pounded the old upright on the porch of his ramshackled home since he was a tot, he wanted that kind of education. He started in half of the games, learned to read music, studied hard at whatever courses came his way, and was pulled into jazz because of a teacher that he admired. He also continued the interest he'd had in boys since childhood, and upon graduation he followed a young man all the way to Paris, where he played in bars for enough money to pay his share of the rent and learned French. The young man left after a while, returning to the states, but The Edge stayed on, took up with a series of lovers, mostly French, and continued to tickle the ivories. He also developed a few drug connections, making small sales of pot to acquaintances for a little profit. He stayed in Paris until his was thirty, then returned to Corpus for a brief stay with his family, which seemed to be falling apart, then headed back to Philadelphia to begin a life there.

Now that football was far behind him, and he'd become a piano player and a drug dealer—he prefers the term "provider"—he called himself Bo, a tough enough diminutive to suit his macho taste and square shoulders. He worked out at an upscale gym three times a week and indulged in deep tissue massages there. For all anyone knew, for he never spoke of his age, he was just a bit over thirty. He didn't consider himself vain, though he was that. He often checked himself out in mirrors. He thought he was a decent enough fellow indeed, but that was questionable.

By the time he reached the corner at Juniper Street, his shirt was soaked with sweat. No matter, he thought, as he turned the corner. There's another at Jack's. Just a few hundred yards to go.

Jack's was already crowded when he opened the door and stepped into the mercifully cool air. Young men sat at tables, a few scattered among the older regulars at the horseshoe bar. The grand piano rested on a riser at the room's end. The light above the keys was turned off, but the imitation brandy snifter, giant-size and empty, picked up light from the dimly lit room. A tip jar he imagined to be half full at evening's end. Well, not evening really, he'd finish at 2:00 am.

He passed among the crowded tables, a few casual hi-fives, some verbal greetings. He smiled and nodded to those he knew. He'd been playing at Jack's, off and on, for a couple of years, Fridays and Saturdays, and he had a following. He sang occasionally. Well, he recited the words in a soft voice as he played the tunes. He was very good with Stardust and other old standards, but not so good with show tunes, though

Jack's clientele often asked for them. Bette Midler numbers, camp tunes from old musicals. These were the younger guys. The older ones requested jazz. Bo didn't care too much either way. He could play most any tune if you hummed a few bars. He liked the job, the easy fellowship, the few trysts that kept him what he thought was healthy. It had been years since he'd had a long term relationship, but he didn't think he missed that. He was just drifting along; good wine, nice clothes, fancy restaurant meals, occasional sex; he wasn't asking for much more.

He crossed the small dance floor, winding his way among couples doing a cheek-to-cheek to sounds of canned Chet Baker coming from speakers at the four corners of the bar. He turned back to look as he reached the storage room door. The crowd looked like a good one, and he felt ready to play. Then he opened the door and stepped inside.

The room was a small one, about the size of a large closet and dimly lit. His locker was next to a stack of liquor boxes, and before opening it, he felt above it for the duffle bag, but found nothing. Curious, he thought, then opened the locker and changed into the clean shirt hanging there.

His first set was a tribute to Paul Simon, something to cross age differences. He stepped up on the riser to light applause and a few friendly calls, turned the light on over the keys, sat down on the bench, and moved into a slow version of *Diamonds on the Soles of Her Shoes*. Then it was *Still Crazy, Mrs. Robinson,* and all the rest, very easy listening and hardly any trickiness with the ivories. Forty minutes later, he finished with *Slip Slidin' Away*. He noted that his snifter was about a quarter full of bills when he got up, turned off the light, and stepped down from the riser to some enthusiastic clapping and a few pats-on-the-back as he moved to the bar and asked for a gin and tonic. He stood there for a few minutes sipping it, then decided he'd better make the call. He plucked his thin phone from his pants pocket, stepped to the end of the bar, and dialed the number. It rang for what seemed a long time, and he was ready to hang up when his party answered, a little breathless.

"Yeah?"

"It's me."

"Hey, B.O.".

"Well, it is hot out tonight. What could you expect?"

Typical banter, he thought, avoiding the issue.

"Yeah, well, there's a little problem"

"I gathered as much."

"Sure. The guy I go to? He says the clamps are down."

"For how long?"

"I don't know, but if I were you, I'd step back for a while."

"I got it," he said. "Take care of yourself."

"Right," he said, and then he hung up.

After his second set, a dozen or so tunes in the style of Bill Evans, Bo passed a few words with Jack's manager. Jack himself was long gone. His sister now owned the place, but she was never there, disapproving, Bo thought, of the gay action. The manager was a little upset that Bo quit, but not much. He shrugged it off, shook Bo's hand, then returned to his office down the narrow hall.

"Have to make a few calls," he'd said.

Bo drank at the bar and thought things over. One more set and that was it. Then what? He opened his phone, went to the end of the bar again, and called his agent. It was after eleven now and, as he expected, he got the answering machine.

"It's Bo," he said. "I'm calling to see if you've got anything. I'll phone you tomorrow morning."

Then he went back to the bench and settled into his final set, those insipid show tunes favored by the younger men.

Chapter 4

RAM CHOPRA

Ram liked to walk along the beach in the early morning, either alone or in the company of Angelo Camp, the manager of the beachfront Sea Burst hotel. He would arrive precisely at 6:00 am, wait for a few minutes on the boardwalk that ran between the closed down amusement park and the beach. If Angie didn't arrive, he'd set off on his own. This morning they were together.

"The beach then, or this wood?"

"Let's do the beach," Angie answered. And so they set out.

It was a beautiful late spring morning, and dusty miller and rugosa roses had begun to bud out in clumps on the low dunes to their left. Terns drifted in the air, gulls sat on the swells, rising and falling, and a few quick pipers pecked for food in the expanse of wet sand revealed as the tide went out. They'd taken their shoes off, and sand squeezed between their toes, a pleasant feeling, as they trudged along.

After a few words, and after they had made their way around a slight turning and the dunes had risen and become high cliffs, the town no longer visible behind them, conversation ceased, and they were left to their own concerns, Angelo's, Ram thought, having to do with the festival that would invade the town come the first of June. He's thinking about his hotel, how he'll handle all those guests, and I'm thinking about the clinic and tooling up for the crowds. All our many little concerns, but it's still a way off.

Ram came to the town six years ago. Shortly after the death of his wife, he'd decided to give up his practice and move east. The job had been listed in medical journals, and he had thought it looked good, and after an interview in front of the town selectmen and a good look at the clinic and its equipment, he negotiated a half decent salary and packed up and moved. He had a small, nicely appointed apartment above the clinic, and he had a recently certified nurse, Melany, in the daytime hours. For the rest of the time he was on call, which was no bother this time of year. Many, if not most, of the townspeople had the use of primary physicians in neighboring towns along the peninsula, and Ram's practice was minimal. His specialty was family medicine, and that fit well with the town's needs. So here he was, in this very relaxed atmosphere, though he was not a happy man. He missed his wife mightily, even after more than six years. He couldn't get beyond his grief, nor his occasionally violent anger. He threw things at the walls, hammered his fists upon the kitchen table, screamed into the night. Thank God they'd had no children. What would he have done then?

Ram was born and raised in India. His family was very well off, rich actually, and he received his medical degree from the University of Delhi, where he studied community medicine with a side line in forensics.

Though his family was saddened by his decision, they provided him with more than ample funds, and he left India for America shortly after his residency, settling in the Midwest, and while working toward certification in this country, he held a position as a morgue assistant in Milwaukee, often knowing more than the coroners who supervised him. When his certification came through, he moved to a large city hospital, and it was there he met his wife, Inder, a nurse who had been schooled in India as well. She seemed to him an intelligent beauty, and after a short courtship they went back to India and were married in a traditional manner, a hundred or more guest, piles of food, dancing in lavish dress. Then they returned to their life and jobs in the city. He was thirty and Inder was twenty-seven. Now Ram was forty-six and Inder was gone. He wore a small silver locket with facing photos ofeach of them inside. It hung from a thin silver chain around his neck.

"What do you think?" Angelo asked. "What kind of stuff might you expect? I remember last year. There wasn't too much."

They had reached a point, a good half mile from town, where the surf drifted into a broad expanse of sand. They could see the Wave Action Study hut near the cliff's edge above. It was familiar to both of them, abandoned and closed up tight, and neither thought anything of it as more than a marker of their progress. They would walk a few hundred yards beyond it, where large boulders sat askew in the sand as they marched down into the surf, then disappeared in the sea. Then they would turn round and head back.

"Maybe some heat exhaustion, dehydration, that kind of thing. Could be a broken bone or two, a few cuts needing suturing. I just hope there are no drownings."

"Good Lord no," Angelo said.

"And you?" Ram said.

"The usual. A full house. Maybe some demanding guests."

"And the party?"

"Oh, yes. For sure. The night before. You're invited!"

"Great!" Ram said, though nothing felt great to him. This was one of those bad mornings. He just kept on walking, feeling his calf muscles flex as the sand fought against his progress.

Exercise was the first thing he tried in order to deal with the loss of Inder and continued at the health club in a town a few miles away. He'd been an athlete in college, football and track, so he found it easy to move into racquetball, work with heavy weights, and, somewhat awkwardly, tennis. It was the effort of the weight training that, in those hours he spent at it, took his mind temporarily away from Inder. He wasn't a bodybuilder, but he worked at strength, honing the muscles in his hands, arms and legs until they seemed as hard as steel. He was lean and wiry, quick on his feet, yet his hands were gentle, and his demeanor, friendly, yet formal, endeared him to his patients.

And while all his concentrated exertion seemed to help, in reality it only poked at his grief, and once he realized this, he returned to that more difficult and grizzly task, the study of his wife's autopsy.

She had been murdered, her body found in a junk-yard, in the backseat of a wrecked Lincoln Town Car, and in the autopsy nothing had been found that linked the victim to anyone but her husband. That itself had been but a momentary awkwardness. He'd been at the hospital seeing colleagues and patients every day, and he was quickly dismissed as a suspect. They had nothing else. But maybe he did, at least he continued to hope so, realizing it was only frustration and rage that keep him going.

He had spoken to the coroner for quite a while and in the end convinced him to hand over copies of the report, pictures of fabric, hair and anything else the crime scene people had gathered. These he kept in a file folder in his apartment above the clinic. Only once could he bear to look at the photographs, but he studied the rest endlessly.

It was almost 8:00 by the time they stepped from the sand and onto the boardwalk. They said the usual as their parting words, though Angie seemed rushed. He had a few guests to attend to. And he was a bit frustrated because of things that weren't spoken of on their walk. He felt very close to Ram. He felt safe in his slight formality, one gentleman speaking to another. And he trusted him with many of his most private concerns and what he thought about them. Today he'd wanted to tell Ram about his current troubles and what they amounted to. He'd wanted to tell him of his confusion. There had seemed no way to introduce these subjects. Then, almost suddenly, their walk had ended.

Ram, for his part, had enjoyed their time together, the small talk, the comfortable silences. Everything soft and civilized. It cushioned those thoughts that were always there, rendering them temporarily manageable. He'd be pleased to get back to the clinic with his home on top. He was indeed pleased when he got there. Melany had made strong Indian tea and had placed a vase of wild flowers on his desk. It was a crisp and sunny morning, a few low billowing clouds; they were very white against the blue.

CHAPTER 5

APHRODITE, 10:30 am

Five foot two. My eyes are blue. I am small, but my heart is big, ha, ha. Yes, I'm that little. Maybe I always looked like a child. Something to explain it. Is it all just a game? What they once called "a cruel joke?" Judging by my pace and aided by that gas station up ahead, I've logged about twenty miles. Not bad, not good. The air seems thinner, here at the top of this low rise I've chugged along a little in ascending. Just a little. Must be residual exhaustion, something from that vigorous late night sex still lingering. I would have called him a hunk, were it not for the flab.

Here at this rise, the sun is intense, its bright light in the stunted scrub at path side and across the way. Cars growl a bit in climbing. A couple of bikers grunt coming by me, then sail free of trouble down the hill beyond. I don't pause, but follow along behind them, watching as they reach the bottom, then bend around a gentle curve and disappear.

What do I look like now?

Blond hair touched with gray, already at thirty-six, tucked under a black cap, the bill pulled down because of the sun. I am trim and very fit. Taut muscles in my arms and legs, a firm flat stomach, hard-won calluses on heels and toes inside my running shoes, Asics. Not all that pretty, my face too much of an oval. Big eyes some find attractive. Little nose. This backpack hangs in comfort along my stiff, muscular, spine. When I walk, I lean a little forward, even when the breeze comes from behind me. Maybe I look intense, or committed. How would I know? I'm the one walking.

I ran track and cross country, in college. Yes, I went to college, Alverno, a Catholic women's school in Milwaukee. It was far enough away from my home town, the house and my father, though I'd say he was in hog heaven when he visited, all those bright young women. I give him his due. He never made a move on anyone, including me. But those eyes. I had to walk out of my dorm room when he came in following dinner. He just sat there, looking. He still seems to be following me, though he's now dead.

In college they called me Aphro, though I of course didn't have one. It was a good reduction of the absurdity of the whole, something I was never called at home. There my father savored my name, speaking it slowly and often, his lingering over it an embarrassment to me, even as a small child, when he used it in front of others.

Cross country was where I felt at ease. We ran in city parks and on roads, dipped into lush woods and meadows when the team went for meets at other colleges and universities. Ours was a city school, but that didn't stop us. We ran and ran, and this took the place of walking. I studied hard, but I was a nervous wreck much of the time: sitting still in classes and lectures, in chapel, shuffling my feet annoyingly at choir, all of it almost an agony, but one that spilled out its stored up energy in running. And there was walking too: around the campus, between classes, in town, on the oval track, in parks nearby. I must have been a sight, four long years, always walking when I could, students waving, laughing, as I walked by. And finally a degree in Physical Education, with a minor in Accounting, which was a mistake. Another mile, and there are dozens more to go. Increased traffic and occasional shops along the way, nature giving in to progress. Fewer tall trees now, and there is the scent of oil in brush along the path.

In college there was occasional meaningless sex, men I met in bars in downtown Milwaukee. Then, after college and a few menial jobs, I walked here, to this peninsula, where I have resided ever since. There's been occasional sexual encounters here, too, but none have turned into what might be called relationships.

For me sex is a matter of memory, orgasm excited not within the sex but with these vivid memory flashes that accompany it: views of my father sitting, my mother bedbound, snatches of bookcases with naked dolls upon them, things like that.

Every image is compartmentalized. A desire for incest? A psychiatrist might name it that. I don't. Just things I have put away, coming back. And there is no nostalgia there either.

The men I sleep with now, including the one I left this morning, are not very interesting. They're a little older, very white and out of shape. They give me nothing but moments of relief. They have my father's eyes.

Okay. There you go. How dramatic. I know: Ned is the installation artist, a funny guy; Bo is the piano player and drug dealer; Ram is the town doctor, obsessed; Lisa is next, followed by two more. Then the tale begins.

Who did you think was telling this story?

CHAPTER 6

LISA JAMES

WHEN LISA LEFT THE COURTHOUSE A FREE WOMAN, she was accosted by the lawyer halfway down the steps. He handed her the divorce papers, told her to have a nice day, then hopped a little sideways as he nimbly descended, much in the way of Fred Astaire in some old musical. Lisa wasn't smiling at these antics, and once she'd reached the sidewalk and begun the long walk to her apartment, she tossed the folder of papers into a trash can in front of some bodega, people milling around behind plate glass. Shit, she thought, and fuck him. That son of a bitch will pay through the nose. He wouldn't of course. She had agreed to the prenup. Still, adultery? Maybe that would nullify things. A different nullification, that of the jury, had set her free.

It was a beautiful early summer day, already quite hot in Tallahassee, but the heat didn't bother her and she walked briskly, passing office workers sitting on benches, smoking and eating lunch-truck meals from plastic containers. She smiled at the ones who looked her way. A mile or more to go, and she lit up one of her Djarums and spent the time going over it once again.

She had married the bastard when she was twenty-eight, just five years ago. Her mother had disapproved because he wasn't a Lutheran. He may have been a Catholic or a Buddhist or anything at all. Her mother never went to church. She seemed to believe in nothing. She liked disapproving. She came to the wedding, but left, to Lisa's chagrin, right after the ceremony: no reception, no wedding present, no smiles and laughter, hugs and kisses. Roger and his family were well off, all of them dandy in dress and manners. They paid for the sumptuous reception, never mentioned her mother's absence, and gave them the gift of a condo in downtown Tallahassee, then left the couple to their own devices. She had called her mother with the news, once she had settled into her new life. Her mother listened, passively; she seemed uninterested, or possibly angry to the core. Lisa had left her mother after all, though she had never actually lived with her.

"Roger bought me a new car, a BMW."

"That's nice."

"We'll be going to Paris for a honeymoon."

"That's nice."

"The condo is beautiful and spacious!"

"That's nice."

That's nice, that's nice, that's nice.

Roger worked in his father's importing business, cheap clothing from Asia and Mexico, just a short walk from home. And Lisa continued with her photography. She had studied the craft in junior college. She was very good at it, and before long, before the marriage, she had established herself as a successful freelancer: weddings and fancy parties and, more importantly for her, auto accidents, fires, candid celebrity shots, and crime scenes. She sold this stuff to newspapers and magazines, and when she had the time she photographed street people and haunting deserted buildings. She'd had a one-woman show at a nice gallery. Everything sold, and at a good price. She was quite content, happy and in love. Then she began to wonder.

Roger had started to go on business trips, flights to Thailand and Mexico. "Just a few days, and I'll be back." She drove him to the airport. He insisted that she not park and come in. "Just drop me outside, at the doors." And this seemed curious to her, and she was a little offended by it, so she called the airlines, faked a certain concern, and found that he was not on the passenger list. Probably a mistake.

Then one day, she herself was to travel to Detroit to photograph an expected union demonstration at some automobile plant. She'd be gone a few days and was excited at the prospect. She packed, got a cab to the airport, only to discover that her flight had been cancelled. She called the newspaper that had hired her and found out that this was okay, she had a day, the demonstration wouldn't happen until tomorrow. Could she get an early flight out? She checked, made another reservation, then headed back home, where she found them.

He had replaced the light bulbs with red ones, had dressed the bed in those purple satin sheets that had been a joke gift from one of his friends, and the furniture had been moved. The large mirror from the foyer had been taken down and placed on the dresser near the bed's foot so they could watch the action. The music was some new-age crap, smarmy piano and strings, and a bottle of Charles Heidsieck and two champagne flutes sat on the bedside table beside the small marble lion that they had bought together at a boutique in town. Nothing seemed left to chance in this tawdry scene, and the first thing she wondered about, but for the champagne, was his taste. And the second thing was the woman.

Was she twelve years old? Petite, fit, and naked, blond hair cut short and shaved up a little above her ears. She was insanely beautiful and almost innocent looking as she gazed at Lisa over his shoulder, numerous studs in her ear, a silver eyebrow ring, her mouth in an O. He was pumping into her, and Lisa wished she had her camera. Then the dam broke.

She moved slowly to the bedside table and lifted the marble lion. He had turned his head and looked at her, seemed about to speak. Then, in her fury, she raised the lion, and swinging her arm high and wide, she brought it down with clear intention, aiming at his head. He lurched to the side, and she missed, striking the woman in the face. Bones cracked and blood squirted from nose and eyes, the spray dappling the lion, her hands and arms. She knew the woman was dead immediately.

She was arrested and charged with first degree murder, but that was quickly reduced to manslaughter, then, through the diligent work of her attorney, involuntary, which would carry a minimum sentence of a year and a half, a maximum of fifteen.

After a few weeks of complaining and bitching, while Lisa sat in jail, her mother agreed to put her condo up as security, and she was released on bail. There was no money. She owed the lawyer a bundle, and Roger and his family came forward with nothing at all. But she had some celebrity, and offers came in from various magazines and TV shows, and she agreed to as many of them as she could handle. It seemed her fame, if that's what it was, had a financial draw. Her byline always mentioned the killing, this crime of passion, her betrayal at the hands of this prominent business man. Then the judge got wind of all this and agreed to the prosecution's gag order. It was close, but she seemed to have made enough money to pay her debts.

After a few months of negotiations there was a trial, which ended in jury nullification. They found her innocent of the charge, and she walked out into the Florida sun and was still walking. She'd be home in just a few more blocks.

The Tallahassee River was on her left, a few boys fishing from boulders at the shore. A hot breeze was blowing now, drying the sweat that had gathered in her armpits. A lukewarm shower is what she needed. Then she'd have to call her mother, listen to that. Then she'd get onto things with her lawyer and that bastard Roger, work up a settlement of some kind. What might work for her was the celebrity, not hers, his. The bastard was already involved with another woman, one of his own "class," and words and lurid photos in the tabloids was not what they needed. She would keep her mouth shut, but it was going to cost him, the dick-head.

"It's over now. I'm free."

"Yes. I know. I heard it on the TV."

"Well?" she said, regretting the word and its begging, as soon as she'd said it.

"Well," her mother said. "Good news."

"Yes," she said.

"But are you ready for the trip? Only a couple of weeks now."

"Yes, of course mother. I'll be ready."

"Is that all then?"

"Yes, I guess it is."

"Okay then. Talk to you soon."

"Right. Goodbye mother."

A bitter taste in her mouth, and she called her lawyer.

CHAPTER 7

CHARLY OLIVARES

Charly and his sister Rosa were walking along the old dirt path, birds in the trees and a rustling in fallen winter leaves, perhaps a vole or some other little forager. It was a way home, the longer way, and they would cut through brush in a half mile, make their way up to the road , then down a block or so to their nice house in Watertown, just a few miles from Boston.

Both carried small backpacks, books and lunch leftovers, and in Charly's a folder of notes and drawings having to do with new tricks he planned to develop and master. A light load for both of them, and they were happy. It was Friday. School was out, not just for the weekend, but for the entire summer. In the fall, Charly, now eleven years old, would enter the sixth grade and Rosa, nine, the fourth. She'd be going to camp for a two week stay this coming Sunday, the day after tomorrow, and Charly, to his delight, would be going with his father to the peninsula and the Day of the Dead celebration. A whole week there. He couldn't wait, not knowing what in particular he would find nor how much room for roaming his father would provide.

His father, Ernesto Olivares, lived in perpetual sadness, something he tried hard to keep from his children. He was forty, a veterinarian who worked in a Boston Animal Hospital near Newmarket Square, and Charly's mother, her name had been Rosa too, had died after giving birth to her daughter almost ten years ago. Ernesto, a very efficient and kind man, had tried hard to pull things together, for his children and their care, even in his profound grief. He'd hired Mrs. Frank, Jeanie to the children, as housekeeper and part time nanny, and much to his relief she'd stayed in the position ever since his wife's death. She cleaned the house and did the food shopping while the children were at school, and then she prepared and cooked dinner before heading for her own home at 5:00 pm.

There were no animals in the house, and this was perhaps an odd thing for a veterinarian. But Ernesto feared for his children's freedom and the attendant animal choirs that might become a burden, transferring his own sadness to them, and though both Charly and Rosa would have liked a puppy, or even a cat, they trusted their father's judgments implicitly. Ernesto and his wife had a dog, a Jack Russell, but she had died shortly after Rosa. Neither of the children remembered the dog, nor their mother. Charly had been a two-year-old, little Rosa but a newborn when she died. There were a few photographs of their mother in their father's bedroom, a small one on the mantle, but no one except Ernesto seemed to look a them. All in all, things were in order in the Olivares's home, though a generally depressing atmosphere remained, even as Ernesto worked hard at cheerfulness in his love for his children. The children, on the other hand, were not depressed. Constantly excited and interested, they were emotionally healthier than their father, resilient in the way children can be, and while they wished, in an almost adult way, that their father had a woman to share his life with, that wish was buried in childhood enthusiasms, and they were unaware of it.

Ernesto was not exactly taking a week off from work to attend the festival with Charly. He'd been hired as an on-call vet by the town. There would be animals in attendance throughout the week, and the town thought it prudent to anticipate accidents and sickness. They'd arranged for housing at a fine old hotel, and Ernesto would carry a cell phone at all times. Problems would be handled through the police. They'd contact him by phone if he was needed.

"Where are the cookies?" Rosa called out as they entered the house. It was beneath Charly to enquire about such things, though he could smell them. Hot from the oven, he thought.

"In here!" Jeanie said from the kitchen, her voice as friendly and welcoming as always. "But wash up first."

Cookies, Charly thought, big deal, though his mouth was already watering. Rosa washed up more quickly than he, and when he got to the table and the plate of chocolate chippers, she was already munching.

"They're hot," she said, chomping away, crumbs falling to the kitchen table. Then she heard the car in the drive, dropped her cookie and ran to the door. "It's daddy! It's daddy!"

For the past few years, ever since I was a little tyke he would have said, Charly had been fussing with mechanical studies in the basement. He'd started with a crystal set, then moved onto locks, taking them apart and figuring out how they worked. After that, it was fishing reels, also dismantled, then studies both in hand and in books he'd acquired, tomes on the many subjects that held his interest. Most recently is was neodymium magnets, their power, polarities and uses. A large metal locker held his wares. It was kept locked so that inquisitive Rosa wouldn't get into his things, although he often entertained her with the various magic tricks he'd perfected. Magic was yet another area that interested him, as was his study of fingerprints. Ernesto had presented him with a kit, and Jeanie would often find remnants of dusting powder on surfaces around the house.

And his father encouraged all this, though at times he wished that Charly would get out more with some friends. He had a few at school, but seldom spent time with them beyond the playground. He was, for the most part, a loner. Always down in the basement or studying in his room, and Ernesto Olivares couldn't fault this. Charly was much like he'd been as a child, though his pleasures had from an early age come from a study of animals. He'd had a bird, a cat, and a dog, and at one point a pet raccoon. And he too had been encouraged by his father. So it goes: fathers and sons.

"We will leave early Sunday morning, after Rosa is picked up by the bus for camp."

Charly grinned, and said "Okay, dad. I'll be packed and ready."

Ernesto thought to say that he shouldn't pack *too* much of his stuff, then had second thoughts. What the hell.

"Bring whatever you need," he said.

"How long will it take?" Charly asked.

"Just a few hours," his father said. "We'll stop for lunch."

"At McDonald's?"

"Sure, why not," Ernesto answered, biting his tongue.

McDonald's after all.

CHAPTER 8

ANGELO CAMP

ANGELO STROLLED DOWN THE BOARDWALK THAT RAN along the edge of the amusement park, between it and the beach. This early morning walk was often taken in the company of Ram Chopra, the town doctor and, as he thought of him, his friend. But not this morning, and Angie was alone with his thoughts.

He was thinking, as he had many times before, that this place was nothing like Bellagio, the small, wealthy Italian town where he had grown up, there on the shore of Lake Como. He had not been a rich kid, but because of his charm had socialized with sons and daughters of the wealthy until he left home for America right after graduation from college. His mother had been a house cleaner, his father an auto mechanic, and both had spoken very good English, learned in time spent in Milan, where they had met, married, had their one child, and then moved back to the Campinelli's modest home outside the small hilly town called The Pearl of the Lake. Angelo's grandparents had died, and the inherited house was comfortable enough for the three of them.

Time went by. Angelo, now known as Angie, had been a slim and attractive boy who had grown into a slim, handsome, distinguished man, and he was still that, though he was now in his early seventies. As a youth he courted the rich girls and befriended the wealthy boys, and when he left for college in Milan, where he studied hotel management, he fell in with a rough crowd for a while, partaking of various drugs and alcohol and spending time in bed with a splendid high school teacher, a little older than him. All this had given him a taste for selective debauchery which he still indulged in from time to time, often in the company of slightly older women.

He was walking, his morning constitutional, along the boardwalk edging the currently placid sea, then up a slight rise at the edge of town and onto a path through the dunes, then down to the bike lane that ran along the highway for his returning. Three and a half miles. It was a beautiful morning. They all seemed to be, and as always he thought about this town he privately referred to as garish and his place in it.

After leaving Milan for America, he bounced around for a number of years through various hotels in New

York City and resorts in the Catskill mountains, working as a bellhop, then night manager, then assistant to top bosses. Eventually he landed a position in Philadelphia, in a large convention hotel where he was the manager. He stayed there for many years, his place of business profoundly affected by various changed in city administrations and their attitude toward conventions. Good times and bad. He was able, through his considerable skills, to weather all the storms, and these abilities ofhis did not go unnoticed.

One day at the height of the season, when he was approaching sixty, he was taken aside by a headhunter, a resident, who was there for a convention at the center a few blocks away, and was asked if he might want to apply for the manager's position at a charming and elegant tourist inn at a beautiful seaside village in Massachusetts. This headhunter was quite beautiful, if a little young for him, and she had been impressed by the manner in which he ran his place.

"I can't imagine that you wouldn't be offered the job," she winked at him. "And the salary is quite good. And the work is much lighter than here."

Maybe she wasn't too young.

He thought it over. He was getting older. The work here was often frenetic and not all that interesting. He might as well give it a shot, at least for an interview, and he was pleased to accept the travel expenses that were offered.

The inn was no inn at all, but a mid-size hotel in a huge old mansion that abutted the beach at the peaceful edge of town. Two dozen elegant rooms, a bar and even a small half circular ballroom with tall windows overlooking the beach and sea, room service, a laundry, and a large manager's office. There was a well-appointed suite provided on the second floor. He studied the kitchen and bar, stood silently in a street side room to judge the traffic and pedestrian noise. There was none. He was offered the job, and he accepted. It was mid-winter when he arrived, and most of the guests were skiers. There was a small mountain that rose oddly and majestically where the peninsula met the mainland, only a few trails and artificial snow, but the town and its lodgings, bars and restaurants were popular, and enough skiers came to keep the place solvent in winter. Once he had moved and was settled in and summer came, that all changed.

Now it was years later, and as he walked the bike path along the highway, he thought of the coming madness, the Day of the Dead, a week-long celebration that had been moved, at the urging of the large Mexican population of hotel workers, fishermen, lawyers, and even city council members, to its original time, that prior to Spanish colonization and the coming of Christianity in the sixteenth century. Now it was early summer, and things would get cooking in just a week.

The rich dilettantes, and the gay men who found the idea campy, and the families with raucous children, and the day trippers and the weekenders, and the drinking and vomiting in the streets, and maybe even a drowning or two. Still, Angie liked his job, this frenetic though easy life touched only occasionally by secret debauchery and a particular self-indulgence that had him in a degree of serious trouble that he chose to ignore as best he could.

It was seven o'clock when Angie got back and checked with Esperanza at the registration desk.

"Just half-full, I see."

"Yes, Mister Camp. The usual this time of year."

"Thanks, Esper," he said, and headed up to his rooms, then called down to the kitchen for his breakfast, coddled eggs, toast and coffee, which was delivered in short order by Lupe.

While he ate he thought about the coming crush. He had a few days to make sure everything was in order. There'd be a new chef coming in tomorrow. He'd interviewed him weeks ago, and tomorrow night he'd go down for dinner, take his measure, though he was quite sure of his skills. Then there were the room cleaners, three new ones, and he'd have to go over things with them. He dipped his toast into his egg coddler and sipped his coffee. Plenty of time. He put his spoon aside, lifted the phone and called Earl, asked him to set up something for tonight, just coke, a little pot, and some women friends.

"Nothing? Well, just the pot then. 8:00? Perfect." Then he got up, went downstairs and walked the half-empty streets of his town.

CHAPTER 9

THE DAY OF THE DEAD

IN THE TRADITION, THE DEAD CHILDREN CAME DOWN from heaven to enjoy the company of their families. Then on the next day the adults arrived, there to party in the town and on the beach and on rides and games and stalls selling various candies and foods in the amusement park. And in bars too and whatever private clubs were available.

The population of the town in winter, forty percent at least from southern and central Mexico, topped out at around three thousand, which swelled to at least ten thousand when *Dia de los Muertos* and the summer itself began.

In the days before the beginning of the festival, new-ly arrived vendors from the old country came with their wares and decorative goods, and many joined forces with the indigenous population in preparing the town for what was to come. Shops along Main Street hung flags and banners in their doorways and set up window displays containing *calaveras*, those skeletal figures representing military and govern-ment personages, as well as farmers, dancers, milk-maids, and many others in bawdy and ironic poses. There were skeleton journalists racing each other on bicycles, heading to make deadlines, skeleton hawk-ers in top-hats wearing sandwich boards announcing world's end in crudely painted figures of disengaged smiling skulls, blustering politicians in tawdry ill-fit-ting suits holding forth on platforms and soap boxes. On the beach, beyond the amusement park, piñatas, cows, dyed dogs, horses, donkeys and other animals, were hung from large balloons filled with helium and tethered to stakes sunk in sand. Once the festival be-gan, vendors would ply the beach dressed in skel-eton outfits, pushing carts fitted with fat tires, selling candy in the shapes of skulls and bones made of mar-zipan and hard black chocolate, wending their way among children and those adults, both vibrant and still half-drunk from the previous night's debauch-eries. And at nightfall there would be bonfires, and mariachi bands, and dancers and jugglers and magi-cians, all dressed in their bones for the occasion, fig-ures bathed in glittering lights from the amusement park behind them, where there would be crowds gathered in abundance, playing games and whooping on rides, swinging chairs, a roller coaster and a Ferris wheel.

The festival began on Monday morning, and through the day a variety of excess could be noted all about the town. The drinking started early, as did the wild machinations of children. Drunks urged them aside, climbing onto water slides and staggering upon entrance into roller coaster cars. Ordinarily subdued mothers paced the beach frantically in fear of their children drowning as they danced into the surf, their mouths full of sugary bones. And the vendors, in constant worry, spread their arms in protection of their wares, candy and costumes and altar preparations, as well as skeleton masks and fake mariachi instruments and sombreros and various other hats for children to use in their festival games. Unicycle riders wobbled down main street, some falling in avoidance of crowds, and shop owners activated door buzzers so as to evaluate those wishing to enter.

It was all a kind of madness, but a somewhat benign one, for it was a celebration of the dead, and even those drunks looking for fights fell into the arms of potential opponents, laughing and dancing. Often they kissed each other on the cheeks and sang old-time Mexican tunes together, as the day moved into evening and the lights in the amusement park and on Main Street provided a friendly glow.

A whorl of many activities pushed the night along, and after a while sounds softened and faded away. A few bars remained open, faint music and talking no more than an aura beyond their closed doors.

Then it was after midnight. The tide was out, and no one walked the littered beach, though a few drunks lounged on blankets far from the edge of the surf. Though the bars would be open for a few more hours, most revelers had retired to their hotel rooms or into sleeping bags or one in a nest of large and small campers at the campground beyond the town. All the shops on Main Street had closed their doors, security lights' reflection turning comic skeleton figures into something a little more sinister behind plate glass. The amusement park had shut down, and its own towering skeletons, those of roller coaster and Ferris wheel, were now only haunting metal rods, beams and joints, massive abandoned Erector Sets faintly visible in the starless sky.

A faint line of phosphorescence where the distant surf rolled placidly out. Darkness, but still a faint light up in the distance, beyond the gradual turn, where the dunes climbed high and became cliffs overlooking the beach. There was a shack up there, the size of a small one room house, and there was a flickering light coming through its one small window, a window that could not be seen through from the outside because of dirt and cobwebs that obscured vision. A sign, its letters faded, was screwed to the buildings side proclaiming that the place was a Center for Wave Action Study, a minuscule center indeed, and one that was clearly no longer in use. There was a door facing the cliff's edge, which after the erosion of recent years was only a few feet away, and above the door handle with its key slot, a new hasp had been screwed into the frame. A heavy padlock hung from the hasp. The door had been unlocked, but there was no sound emanating from inside, only that flickering dim light suggesting occupancy. Then the light was snuffed out, like the lives of the dead, and the first day's revels of *el Dia de los Muertos* ended.

On Sunday evening, the night before the festival began, Angelo Camp hosted a small, private, inaugural ball at his hotel. Invitees dressed in the bones they had brought with them, and some who were last minute arrivals purchased their outfits in shops on Main Street. Bo Bogardus was one of them, having arranged for an invitation through his agent. He'd driven to the town from Philadelphia instead of flying. He'd brought some goods with him, thinking he might sell something here and there. And he'd hit the mark almost immediately, connecting up with Angelo.

He was standing off to the side in the small ballroom, attempting to look less than ridiculous in the skeleton jumpsuit he'd picked up at a costume store in the city. A top hat came with it, and because there seemed no place to put it down, after tapping it against his leg and pressing it against his chest, he put it on. His drink was a Beefeater's martini, and that itself, in its appropriate glass, seemed to him comic—a skeleton holding such a thing.

He had tried to mingle, but found few guests to his liking. He'd spoken to a handsome fellow who appeared quite ridiculous in skeleton gloves and bony spats worn at both ends of rough wear: corduroys too bulky for the weather and a wrinkled tan silk shirt that looked quite expensive. They passed a few words, both awkward in their getups. His name was

Ned, and after their brief conversation—the weather, the fine hotel rooms they both occupied—Bo moved away to speak with a lovely looking woman named Lisa, who managed to maintain her dignity, even in a T-shirt depicting an x-ray of her ribs and classic girdle. And the town doctor was there, as well as a veterinarian who dipped into conversations in the elegant little ballroom for only a few minutes before leaving.

This room is indeed elegant, Bo thought: cherrywood flooring laid out in an intricate pattern; tall, broad windows, through which the sand and sea were close at hand; and off to his left, where he stood apart, a gently curving mahogany bar, behind which row upon row of liquor bottles glimmered in indirect light and a tall, thin skeleton parceled out a variety of drinks.

Then Angelo approached Bo, the good host, seeing that he was alone.

"You're alone?" he said.

"Yes," Bo answered. "All alone. I arrived this afternoon. I'm staying here."

"Ah," said Angelo. "This is my hotel, you know."

"You're the owner? A very nice place."

"No, no! I'm the manager."

"Ah," Bo said.

And so it continued. Small talk. Then in a while, as Bo often found with potential customers, the conversation got around to drugs, and the connection was made—four gramsof coke at a very good price.

"Seems fair," Angelo said. "Tomorrow morning?"

Only then did Bo let it be known, to Angelo's surprise and laughter, that he'd be the piano player in the hotel bar come tomorrow night.

CHAPTER 10

APHRODITE, 2:00 pm

Sometimes I imagine my father is in my backpack, naked and small as one of those ludicrous dolls he was so fond of. He's tucked in there, and even though I might walk quickly, he is still present, always following.

Still a few hours to go, and I'm feeling a renewing of energy, like a horse heading back to the stables for supper. I too will eat something once I arrive and before I start back, a sandwich and a bottle of water picked up at a gas station or food mart in the town. I'll return in the night, when all the world is asleep but me. I like the feeling of the dark.

After my father had been declared dead and his will had been probated, and this took quite a while, seven long years actually, I flew back to Wisconsin to deal with the house and the things in it. I of course walked the aisles of the plane, rising and setting off when the seat belt light was out. It was hard going, sitting there for takeoff and landing, but I felt I was too old now for walking that long distance as I had earlier. I did walk from the airport to the house, to "stretch my legs" you might say, though they were well stretched already. How many miles have I logged? Impossible to say, for I've never kept that kind of accounting.

The police had been to the house and had found the brief suicide note my father had left on the kitchen table. They'd gone there since his clothing and identification had turned up on rocks at the shore of lake Winnebago. Winnebago is a large lake, thirty miles long and ten wide, but it is shallow, running to a depth of just over twenty feet, and the police and coroner's office had become curious, since, though they had dredged and employed divers, they hadn't recovered my father's body. That was in the past though, and he has since been declared dead.

It must be close to 3:00 pm. Five hours at least until sunset.

The house was musty, since it had been closed up tight for years. My father's lawyer had seen to that, and he was the one who had contacted me when the declaration of death went into effect. He'd left a letter, in a sealed envelope with my name carefully penned in, on the kitchen table, together with his phone number and address on a Post-it. The letter was from my father, and I have since read it many times and have memorized it. There was a large key, too, in the envelope. This is what the letter said.

My Dear Aphrodite,

Long time no see. And yet I have missed you, though I am beyond such missing now. When you read this, I will be gone, and at my own hand.

I've left the house to you, everything in it, and the money, as well as my dolls.

When you go through the place, you'll come upon painful things. They'll be an embarrassment to me, but please don't think too harshly of me, if you are able. I'm sorry to put you through this, my dear child.

I've attached a list of names, trustworthy individuals from this and nearby towns. They can deal with the furniture and carpets, the artwork, the kitchen ware and the painting and minor repair of the place, so you can put it on the market. Two names are those of doll merchants. I trust them, but only so far. Get independent appraisals and get receipts. And last of all, the real estate agent. She's a very good one, smart and tenacious. She'll get the place sold in a jiffy.

And once all this is done, you'll be free, truly free. At least I hope so.

Now it is time to end this letter, dear Aphrodite, but before I do there is something I want to set straight, if it needs setting straight, for I suspect that a lifelong misunderstanding may have occurred between us.

As you know, how could you not know, though I have tried to be discrete about it, I was a sufferer with childhood diabetes. There were shots and pills to be taken; there were occasional skin blemishes. What you don't know, for I have kept it secret, is that from early on, even since you were no more than three years old, I'd been treated for diabetic retinopathy, a condition whereby my sight was often confused. And this, over the years, was followed by a degree of macular edema, a condition that can lead to blindness.

I had looked at you, my child, as things progressed and my sight slowly worsened. I did not want to lose you, the image of you, so I followed you from room to room, always gathering your face and holding it close, even as you became, more and more, a shadow figure.

I suspect you saw it otherwise, that I desired you in a way a father should not. This is not true. I loved you as my child and only wished to hold you, as long as possible, in my gaze.

And so it was, Aphrodite. My sight worsened, your dear mother, my wife, left me for death, and I was all alone, with only the promise of a cane and dark glasses in my future. I knew blindness was soon coming, so I decided to leave.

Now it's goodbye my dear. Please forgive
me for any perceived wrongs. I loved you. I
would still, were I able.

Your father, Rodney Appell

*The goofy formality of the language, the thoughtful prepa-
rations designed to make things easier for me, the too few
sad words about my mother, and then, of course, the outra-
geous, almost comic, explanation of that gaze that set me off
to walking.*

*I read the letter through a couple of times, and then I set
out to select those things I might keep and take back with
me. There was nothing, not in any of the rooms, so I went
down into the basement to look there. The dioramas, the
doll figures and parts, the small tools, and the cage that
had held that mad monkey, abandoned now. Then I went to
the locked door tucked in behind the boiler, inserted the key
that had been in the envelope, and looked into the small,
forbidden, room.*

*It was at first as if I was facing a stall at a comic book
convention. The bold doll caricatures painted and stenciled
upon the cement walls assaulted me even in the dim light
behind me. There was a switch beside the wall, and when I
turned on the bare light bulb that hung from a cord in the
ceiling, what had seemed at first comic turned into something frightening and forbidding.*

*A life-size rubber doll, not a pornographic sexual aid,
but a large rendering of the naked doll figures my father
worked with. It hung from a hook attached to the wall, a
rope fastened around its neck, and its abdomen and chest
had been thrust through with a butcher knife and a sword,*

and the tips of its breasts had been hacked away. There was no expression at all on its doll face. To me it represented the figure of a tortured saint.

And there was more that hinted of torture. A waist high metal shelf attached to the wall was suspended to the side of a gynecological stirrup table. I approached it and saw the blood spatters below where the legs might be suspended. There was blood on the walls too, and on the shelf was a gathering of instruments, larger versions of the ones my father used in his doll dressing and repair. There was a sheaf of notes on the shelf too, and I fingered through them—drawings of naked women in various posture, and a list of things that might be done to them. It was disgusting, and I quickly closed the folder and tucked it under my arm. I'd looked at only a few pages, but that was enough.

I left the room and its depictions and devices and searched the basement for flammable liquid. I found acetone and a large can of solvent, then went back to the room and splashed both over the objects and the walls. There was a vent high on one wall, and I trusted that it would release whatever dangerous gas might be emitted and would provide air. The room, including the ceiling, was constructed of cinder block and tight cementing, so I was in no fear of the fire spreading to the rest of the house. Then I took a box of kitchen matches, lit a few and cast them and the box itself into the horrifying little room. It took a few moments, then flames rose from the table and the legs of the large doll figure. I waited a few moments, then closed the door. It fit quite tight, and only a little smoke seeped out around the frame.

How late could it be now, 3:30, 4:00? I've lost track of my pacing. The sun is still quite high. I should reach the town before nightfall, maybe a little later. It doesn't matter.

I have thought of that room and its implications for a long time now. What could my father have been thinking? Why did he leave the room for my discovery and not destroy it as I had? And I have thought often of my father's letter too, only to scoff at it. This time though, in thinking it through once again, I begin to feel a certain sadness and love for my father. Maybe the business about his vision was the truth. Maybe he really did love me. Oddly, I feel I could forgive all the rest, if I had that love.

After a week in the house dealing with things, I gave over the sale of the place to the agent my father had recommended. He was right, she was quite good. And I called the lawyer, then went to talk with him, and settled things. The house would soon be painted and the repairs made. The gutted room would be cleaned of rubble, then sealed up with cement. I left all this to the contractor whose name was on my father's list. Then I loaded my backpack with the few piece of clothing I'd brought with me,the folder of notes and one of my father's shirts. Time to go. Once again I flew. Once again I walked the aisles.

CHAPTER 11

MONDAY

NED AWOKE TO THE SOUND OF FROLICKING VOICES, then staggered naked to the gauzy curtains on his painful feet and pulled them apart. Out on the beach a volleyball game was underway, twelve young men in curious costumes, half blonde, the others sleek brunettes, some shaved close above the ears. Half wore speedos in the shape of skulls, white on black. When these tanned and muscular bodies danced about in the gaming, their skulls briefly came alive, cheeks in gyration, contorted mouths. The other half wore skeleton suits in various lurid colors. These looked painted on their hard thin bodies, bones clacking silently in ecstatic movement.

The game continued. The score seemed close. The expended energy of the young men became more vivid. Lithe bodies dove for the ball like elegant arrows, landing in sand that puffed up in circus sawdust along their arms and legs. Some leapt high into the summer morning, spiking the ball hard across the net.

Then, in a while, the game ended in laughter and good fellowship, and the losing team ducked under the net, rushing to embrace the winners. Their sweating bodies pressed tight against each other, hands caressing shoulders and hips. Some danced in place, while other couples fell into the sand, wrestling and rolling about, their calls joyfully audible in the crystal air.

Ned let the curtains fall, unaware of how long he'd been standing there, his body heated by the sun that warmed the glass. Then he turned and went back to his bed and sat on the edge of it and swore at his feet.

After he'd showered and shaved and fussed with his hair and doused himself, here and there, with his Hugo Boss cologne, he looked at the suit that lay across the bed. He didn't wear suits, though he lifted this one and worked to get himself into it. His shirt collar felt stiff. His tie remained askew.

The hell with this, he thought, knowing he'd look like a fool in formal attire, out there among the partying tourists and those dancing around in their bones. But his mother had insisted, so what could he do. Maybe he could find a skull mask somewhere.

Ned had arrived at the Sea Burst in the late morning of the previous day. He'd found an invitation waiting in his beautifully appointed room, mid-Victorian in style with a very modern bathroom. He was invited to a party in celebration of the coming festival, The Day of the Dead. It would be hosted by the hotel manager, who had signed the invitation and added a handwritten note at the bottom saying "bones are required." What the hell, he thought, why not.

Then he wondered what he'd do with the intervening hours; there were plenty of them. So he called room service and asked them to put together a little picnic lunch, just a sandwich, a piece of fruit, and a soda. He hadn't been into the center of town, but instead of walking there, he crossed to the beach, where the volleyball court was now empty, then headed along the beach and away from the town. He walked close to the surf where the sand was hardest; the tide was on the way out, and his pathway became increasingly easier. He'd taken off his shoes and socks and had rolled his khakis to the knees, and his feet were feeling better. It was a pleasantly warm summer morning, and its softness seemed untouched by the drunks Ned passed in his slow progress. They lay in the sand like long dead and corrupted bodies, drained now to their skeletons, those outfits stained by putrid vomit and occasional flecks of blood. Half empty whiskey bottles rested close to their bony fingertips.

Ned found a place for himself on a broad, shallow rock that had been smoothed by sea and wind. The rock was shaded by the rising dune behind it, and beyond the shade the sun was slightly subdued, the sea placid and as deeply blue as the sky above. He took out his lunch, spread it on the large linen napkin provided by the Sea Burst and proceeded to eat and give thought to things that had nothing to do with his mother's impending wedding. It was his art that concerned him.

What should he do? He couldn't do nothing. He should have recognized what was happening. His installations had been getting more and more repetitive, at least to his eye now, and he'd been losing interest. The reviews and photograph sales had kept him from looking closely at what he was doing. He wasn't doing much, certainly nothing that gave him satisfaction any more.

Why not painting? He had painted quite seriously in his youth, and he thought he might even have been good at it. It might be a start anyway. And here. There were plenty of subjects to consider, all these boned up people, the amusement park, even this beach here. He could draw them. He was good at drawing. And then, later, he could try to paint picture from these drawings. Day after tomorrow, he thought. I'll pick up some paper, charcoal and sketch pencils.

When he reached the town hall, which was smack in the center of town, he worked his way through the crowd of revelers, climbed up the steep cement steps and entered the place. Looks like some kind of old mansion, he thought. A large open foyer, paintings of old time judges on the walls. He went to the desk and was told that weddings took place upstairs, third room, number six, on the right. He climbed up the stairs and came to a wide hallway, a row of doors on either side. And there was six, a silver number on the heavy mahogany. He pulled it open, it took some effort, and entered into a large, bare room in which his mother stood, dressed in her wedding outfit. She wore a sleek white sheath adorned with large calla lilies, high heels, and a little pillbox hat cocked slightly to the side. Beside her was another woman, this one much younger and dressed as he was, appropriate to the occasion. He moved quickly up to his mother and reached out to embrace her. She pushed her palms out to ward him off, then spoke in her cross voice.

"It's over."

"Over? Over!," Ned said. "You mean I missed it?"

"No, dummy! Not the wedding. The relationship! The wedding's off."

Ned was stunned. He didn't know what to say.

"I don't know what to say," he said.

"Yeah, sure. Neither do I. And by the way," she tilted her head to the side, "This here is your sister."

The younger woman shifted on her feet, clearly uncomfortable.

"My sister? My sister! What in the hell are you talking about?"

"Language!"

They went for lunch at a little place across the way. It was crowded, but they managed to find a table off in a corner. There were *calaveras* all around them, both those that were children and adults, but most of the bones remained stationary, linked to mouths that were intent on the quick devouring of their food, for the most part pizza and burgers, though Ned and his family settled in with soup, salad, and grilled cheese.

It was like this. The intended had arrived at the hotel disheveled and drunk and in the company of two new drunken "friends" that he had picked up at a bar in the town. Edna Hobby had been ready for some billing and cooing before they headed out to the ceremony, but none of that was forthcoming.

"Drunk!" she said. "I threw the bastard out!"

"Maybe he was nervous and all. Things like that," Ned said.

"Oh, bull shit!" his mother answered, and skulls turned from their feasting, though temporarily, and looked over at them.

"Now mother," Lisa said.

Lisa, sheis my sister, Ned thought. What about that?

After Ned had left home for good, Edna had become pregnant, though she had no wish for another child. She had a sister who had such a wish, and had farmed Lisa out to her, keeping in close touch, but free of the necessary caring, diapers and things, those adolescent troubles. It had gone quite well, and when her sister had died, Lisa was already out on her own, earning a living, and in no way depended on Edna's largess. This seemed quite perfect to Edna, and the two remained just a little more than friends, though Lisa might well have wished for more.

Ned kept looking over at her where she sat across the table. Something vaguely familiar about her.

"Where you at Dad's funeral?" he asked. "And didn't I see you at the hotel party last night?"

"Yes, I was, Ned. At Both. But Edna didn't want me to announce myself at the funeral." Though she called Edna mother and sometimes mom, it didn't seem quite right to use such terminology right then. Ned seemed to get that, but he didn't get the rest.

"So, why didn't you ever tell me? I had a sister after all. I deserved to know."

"Deserved?" Edna said. "And I didn't deserve to be abandoned by my son?"

"I didn't abandon you. I saw you in New York. A couple of times."

"Right. A couple of times in close to forty years!"

She was right about that, of course, and once again Ned found himself in the wrong.

"But my sister," he said, almost whining.

"Get over it," Edna said in her practiced icy voice.

"So we're staying at the same hotel, the Sea Burst," he looked across the table at Lisa, avoiding his mother's hard eyes.

"We all are," Lisa answered.

"All?" he said, looking back at his mother. "You're there too? Why didn't you tell me?"

"Enough interrogation," Edna said. "I'm going down to the beach."

"How long will you two be staying here. I mean, now that the wedding's off?" He was trying to lift the conversation into a bit of congeniality. It didn't work.

"Long enough," Edna said, as she rose from her chair.

At around the same time, near noon on the first day of the festival, Ram Chopra sat at his desk in his apartment above the clinic, eating his lunch, toasted Swiss and ham on rye, and a glass of Arizona iced tea. He could hear the faint sound of voices below him and knew it was Ernesto Olivares, the veterinarian he had agreed to share one of his examination rooms with for the Day of the Dead week. Ernesto seemed a good man, and at Angelo's party they had spoken about the loss of their wives, almost at the same time, a few years ago. In only a few minutes, they had made a close connection. Ram had met someone else at the party, one Lisa James, and thinking of her was giving him some trouble. He couldn't seem to concentrate.

He could see out to the street through a window that faced his desk. The clinic was back on a side-street, no shops of interest, and no restaurants or bars. And yet there was music emanating from small devices and a dozen or more festival dancers cavorting about. No containers of booze that he could see. Just fun loving escapades. Derbies and smiling skulls, a devil or two, and a couple of angels, escorts for the dead children coming down. They wore raggedy Papier-mâché wings and nun like wimples. They reminded Ram of parade costumes from his childhood in India. Universal madness, he thought. But it does look like fun. He took a bite of his sandwich and glanced at the file folder and the thick stack of autopsy material that rested beside it.

A few weeks following his wife's death, when his grief had cooled a little and been replaced by a hot rage, Ram had begun his study of the autopsy report and the photographs of his wife's clothing and other items gathered by the crime scene investigators. Then, off and on, over the next few years, he had gone back to his study again and again. There were long periods when he put the materials aside and concentrated on his medical work, reading the current journals. This would sustain him for a while. Then a certain emptiness would come upon him, and he would spread out the materials, most usually on the desk where he now sat eating his lunch. He looked over at the folder and the stack of papers. Then he looked out the window once again. The revelers were gone, the street empty. He could hear the distant sounds of the festival, white noise only at this distance. Nothing to do.

Lisa James. She was a little younger than he, but not that much. She had glorious blond hair and a slim, solid figure that maintained its curves even in the skeleton getup she had worn to the party. He'd been dressed in a dark suit and a skull mask: the grim reaper, though he carried no scythe. He thought he might have frightened her a little when he approached. He did look a bit scary. But he'd made a light joke of some sort. He couldn't remember what he'd said. And this seemed to calm her. They laughed a little, spoke only briefly, then joined with others at the celebration. When he looked around, hoping to talk to her again, she was gone, too soon. He thought he was going to try to find her. He'd check with Angie. It shouldn't be hard. Then guilt descended upon him, for he felt he was betraying his dead wife.

The dog nipped at the cat that was after the rat, and the cat turned and attacked the dog's nose, whereupon he leapt back and fell into the bog and was bitten on the leg by a snapping turtle that held on until the man whacked it in the head with a fallen limb.

This all took place at the campground, well away from the festival doings, and now the furry little devil was held down by the man, on the treatment table in Ram Chopra's clinic, while his two children wept beside his diminutive wife and Charly Olivares looked down at the dog intently as his father applied a local anesthetic, then inserted a few sutures into the gash below the dog's knee, where he'd shaved the hair away. Then he bandaged the wound, looked up at the father and said, "That's it." The father lifted the dog then, up from the table and into his arms, and the family departed, leaving behind a profusion of emotional thank yous.

"So that's it," Charly said.

"Right you are," Ernesto answered. Now why don't you skedaddle. Get some of that fibula candy, take in a ride or two? But Charly, only the shallow water. You have your phone?"

"Yes, Dad."

"Okay. A couple of hours? I should be back at the room. But call me if you need anything."

"Okay." He waited.

"That's it!" his father laughed. "You can hit the road." And Charly left.

It was already mid-morning, and Angie was shaking in his boots, though he still wore his slippers. I must get downstairs, he thought, the place is full, the festival is underway. The new cook, Bo, the piano player, the guests.

He'd received the call at 6:00 am. He was still sleeping, and when he answered, thinking it was some hotel problem, he was groggy, the celebration party, the drugs and that other party the night before.

"Yes?" he said.

"Time is running out, Mister Camp. Very quickly."

"Who is this?" Though he knew quite well who it was.

"Enough of that. You have until mid-week. Let us say Thursday. That's all you have."

"Of course," Angie said, trying hard to sound civilized. He might have said more, but the line went dead.

He'd been gambling heavy for the past year, winning and losing, mostly losing. It was an old story. He knew that. And the drugs too, that had cost him. And that led to the loan sharks at Foxwoods. They were there always, looking for easy pickings, and they'd picked him. Now it was thousands of dollars, money he didn't have and nowhere to turn. He must speak with Ram. Get some sound advice.

He'd gotten up and called down for his breakfast, and while eating he'd gone through the Sea Burst's books, something he did weekly, though this time he was looking for something other than balancing. Was there a way? Could he borrow something. Good Lord! He thought. Stealing? He wouldn't do that. His relatives in Bellagio? Forget it. They were all gone now, but for a few cousins and their kids.

He moved around in his rooms, pacing between the windows and the furniture, thinking, coming up with nothing. Then he dressed and went downstairs and checked with the new cook and Esperanza at the desk. Bo was at the piano in the lounge, dressed in linen shorts and a silk T-shirt, checking the instrument's action. Angie listened as he played a few bars of *Here's that Rainy Day*. Very nice indeed, Angie thought, then he went to the hotel phone and called Ram Chopra.

Lisa and Ned walked back to the Sea Burst together. The streets were crowded and noisy, kids and adults, mid-day drunks, and a unicycle rider who almost clipped them. All were in costumes, or parts of them, and they were jostled into sideways stepping from time to time. So they headed away from Main Street, where it was quieter, and as they passed by the doctor's clinic and Lisa gazed up at the apartment above it, Ned urged her into her life story and she took interest in his. Neither story had been passed on by their mother, so everything was new to them.

She told him of her photography, a few of the many celebrity shots, then of her aunt, his aunt too, that had raised her. And finally she got to her marriage, her husband's infidelity, and the killing she had been tried for. His story seemed to pale in comparison, though he told it, mustering as much enthusiasm as he was able. She was interested in his art, he in hers, and by the time they reached the Sea Burst each felt like sister and brother, and they hugged and kissed in the lobby, then headed up to their respective rooms, where Lisa gathered up her photographic equipment and Ned put on his swimming suit, his khakis over it. They left separately, both heading back into town and the amusement park and the beach beyond it, Ned thinking of his upcoming drawing, Lisa thinking of a certain doctor.

Edna Hobby was not an unattractive woman. Of medium height, she was compact and thin, had very good legs, and her greying hair, while short, was quite sexy in its modern severe cut. She exercised daily and was in very good shape. She looked quite a bit younger than her seventy-three years. She was unaware of all this, and because of that seemed to be without annoying ego. She never looked at herself in the mirror, which was a good thing, for she might have been shocked at how her pretty face so often took on the shape and corrugated structure of a prune. She was perpetually angry, and this she was not unaware of. After all, her son had abandoned her, as had her husband, leaving her with a daughter she had never wanted. And now this drunken bastard! Shit-faced on the brink of their marriage! *Fuck him! Fuck them all!*

She sat on her blanket on the beach as far away from the frolicking children as she could get, which wasn't far enough. The beach was crowded, but at least there were no drunks nearby. She sat where a family area had been staked out by the presence of families, and the liquored up bastards stayed away. But these stupid noisy kids! Just look at these pains in the ass, splashing around, yelling and throwing sand at each other! Then she caught herself. Wait just a minute, she thought. They aren't Ned, they aren't Lisa, they aren't my husband or that drunken fool. They're just kids having fun. Look at them. Her prune face relaxed then, the wrinkles flattening out, and she began to smile and nod at their behavior. What is wrong with me? she thought, feeling a little sad, though more relaxed than she'd been in quite a while.

They seemed to like each other, my two children, though they had never met. And Ned hadn't even known of her existence. I'd kept it from him. Why? Who would have wanted to come visit an old battleaxe like me after all? Of course he'd kept away. I would have. Oh, son-of-a-b, maybe *I'm* the asshole.

And this quick and uncalled for revelation stunned her. She breathed in deeply, leaning back in her beach chair, then breathed out all the poison and cancerous anger that had controlled her. At least for now, she thought, as she closed her eyes and felt the mild sun warm her relaxed brow. Sleep, she thought, and in moments fell into it.

She woke as the sun was blocked out by shadow, and when she opened her eyes, he was leaning over her, a young boy with dark curly hair and brown skin, a look of concern on his face.

"Are you okay?" he asked in a gentle voice.

"Yes, yes. I'm fine, just fine," she answered in a dreamy whisper.

"You were so still," he said. "I was worried."

"Really?" she said. "I'm okay. Better than usual. What is your name?"

"Charly," he said, rather shyly.

"Charly," she said. "Why don't you sit down here for a while?"

And without any urging or coaxing, he immediately did what she requested. He plunked himself down on his towel in the sand beside her, then began talking, in a measured and slow way.

"Olivares," he said. "Charly Olivares. I'm here for the week with my father. He's a veterinarian. His name is Ernesto. He's here to care for the animals. This morning it was a snapping turtle bite."

"What did the turtle bite?"

"Oh," he said. "I didn't say. It was a dog, a little one."

"My goodness," she said.

What a handsome lad she thought.

"And you. What do you do?"

"Well," she said. "I was a nurse, I worked in surgery. People, you know? But now I'm retired. I'm here with my son and daughter. A vacation."

"It's a real madhouse," he replied. "But a lot of fun too!"

"I'll bet it is," she said. "And Charly, what do you do?"

"Do? Well I'm in school you know. I'll be entering the sixth grade. But I do other things as well.

"Oh?" she said.

"Yes. Things with locks and keys. With magnets too. And I also do magic and fingerprints."

"Will you do one for me?"

"What?"

"A magic trick," she said.

"Well, okay," he answered, smiling his charming smile. "But I only have these cards. So here," he offered the fanned deck. "Pick any one."

They sat there in the sand for a long time, talking of various things, casually and at times intensely, then back to the casual once again. Edna was soothed by his frank, unaffected voice, his various interests, his love for his sister and father. Perhaps Ned and Lisa might have loved her, perhaps they did. She spoke in some detail about her work as a surgical nurse, told him about her son and daughter, that he was an artist, she a photographer. She bragged about them, but not expansively. And in awhile she fell in love with him, this little boy who had shown concern for her, that she might be ill. She loved his look and his manner, and she wanted more of him.

As the sun moved into the afternoon and the sky grew blue, mothers and fathers packed up their beach gear and their children and headed back to their various lodgings, and all remaining sounds, those of distant celebration, came from the town and the amusement park in the distance. They made a plan. They would meet again, in a few days. He would bring more of his magic tricks and other things. She would bring sandwiches and drinks.

Ned's nipples were licked by the shushing spray as he sailed down the water slide and splashed into the pool at the bottom. His swimsuit had slipped and he struggled to pull it back up, then was hit by the body of boy who had yelled out "Move!" as he came down behind him. Once again he experienced splash down, then struggled to his feet again and this time moved to the side moments before another boy sailed up in the air beside him and cannon-balled into the pool.

Ned shook the water out of his ears, then moved cautiously to the other side, and as he was preparing to climb out, he saw a man standing on dry ground watching him. He was tall and lean and very nice looking, and Ned, surprised at himself, found him quite attractive.

The laughter of the children, the slosh of the water in the pool, the crank of the Ferris wheel, and the call of the vendors, all this faded and became white noise. The sun shimmered on his shoulders and in the space between him and the man he was heading for. It was as if Ned was wading up to his ankles in a cloud like those depicted in romantic visions of heaven. He pulled his suit up once again, smiling coyly as he approached.

"Hi, there," he said. I'm Ned."

The taller man looked down at him, grinning.

"I'm Bo. We met at the party."

"Oh, okay. Great. Nice to see you again. Do you think I could draw your picture?"

Right then, without further adieu, they became a couple.

"Ah, Ms. James," he said. "Isn't that it? Come in, come in!"

"It's Lisa," she said. "Please call me Lisa."

She had walked the streets of the town, taking a few shots, buildings and people, but she found little that interested her. Too much frenetic activity, no real drama, and when she dipped beyond the crowds onto side streets where there were no celebrants, but only a few merchants and home owners, she found herself standing in front of the medical clinic. She remembered the doctor, wasn't his name Ram? A nice name, though a tough one, and before she knew it she was standing in front of the reception desk, and the nurse was speaking quietly on the intercom. In only moments, he came out and greeted her. He was wearing a white smock, his glasses hung from a black cord and bounced lightly on his chest as he approached.

There were no human patients, only those of the veterinarian who shared the office, a dog and a sheep—a sheep? She thought—and after removing his smock he took her up the back stairs to his quarters, into the small office, then, while she adjusted the Venetian blinds in order to dim the space and let in shadows, he left her and quickly returned in a few moments only, wearing a fine, black linen shirt. He'd combed his dark hair.

She placed him in a chair near the window, so that light fell in narrow ribbons of shadow across his chest and face. A few haunting shots. She had a way of taking a great deal of time in adjusting her subjects when it came to portraiture, the placement of arms, the tilt of head. Then she would get ready, and sighting through the camera would pause for too long a time before shooting. She wanted just a bit of discomfort, an expressiveness that came from anticipation for a climax that was momentarily withheld. She could see his brief concern, that attractive intensity she'd wanted, there in his slightly tensed forehead, his focused eyes. She pressed the shutter release, again and again, and when she noticed there were only a few frames left on the roll, she went to where he now stood, arms folded across his chest, legs crossed at the ankles. He was leaning back against the wall, and she wanted him standing erect, shoulders back, his chin thrust slightly forward.

The space between them was no more than a few feet, but when she lowered the camera, she saw that the rug was patterned by shadows and those ribbons of light that undulated as low thin clouds passed before the sun, dimming it, then gleaming through. The rug now seemed three dimensional, as if it were a thick topographical map of some landscape in a dunned desert. She stepped into it, her feet seeming to sink in, and moved slowly to where he stood. It took her a long time. When she reached him, she raised her hand to his cheek, intending to turn his head slightly. He reached for her wrist, held it, then looked into her eyes. Could this be paradise? she thought, as he pulled her into his body. Then he kissed her, deeply, and in minutes that seemed seconds, he turned her and led her away from the wall and the window and into the bedroom where there was a more constant sunlight, few shadows, but a slight shimmering on the bedspread that had been neatly tucked in and mitered at the bottom corners.

On Tuesday morning, after Ernesto had left for the clinic, Charly packed a blanket and a towel in his backpack and headed down to the beach at town center to practice his card shuffles. He had mastered the simple things, the riffle and the one hand cut, and was now into more difficult manipulations, the various cascades and the tricky Sybil, a complex fake shuffle designed to confuse observers.

It was only 8:00 am, but the beach was already crowded, children playing to the warm surf, Day of the Dead early risers in their skeleton costumes. It was noisy, and the more Charly shuffled the more frustrated he became. He had to *hear* the cards, but there was too much laughter and splashing, so he packed up his gear and headed down the beach, past the Sea Burst, until he came upon a broad flat rock the size of two card tables at some casino. There were a fewboulders buried in the sand nearby, but there were no people. The sun was bright, rising up out of the placid sea, the tide at that point of stasis between high and low. Charly put on his sunglasses and his cap, spread the blanket over the rock's surface, and began his work, flexing his fingers and listening to the pleasant sound of the cards movements. He was getting a handle on the Sybil, intent in his practice, and only became aware of the other when he was no more than thirty feet away.

"Excuse me," the man said, and Charly looked up and watched him as he slowly approached.

He was a heavy man, shorter than Charly's father, and his legs looked spindly below his baggy cargo pants. An old man, Charly thought, and though he walked with a cane and his bare feet sunk into the sand, the cane tip barely touched the surface. He's not really using it, thought Charly. And that shirt. It was black, the wrong color for the summer season, and it absorbed rather than reflected the bright sunlight. There were dim, monstrous animal figures printed or sewn into it, twisted carnivores, like those in some Hieronymus Bosch paintings, the ones Charly had studied carefully in one of his father's art books. These figures, a unicorn with a bloody spike, a snarling wolf like dog, a man with the legs of a goat stained with the entrails of some eviscerated, screaming bull-like figure he had trod upon. The man was smiling, his wet lips lifted at the corners, his pencil line mustache twitching. He was almost bald and had combed his few hairs forward to cover his broad forehead. It looked silly, and Charly removed his sunglasses and then saw the steel glint in the man's eyes.

"Do you mind if I join you?" He said, his voice somewhat high, yet as smooth as melting butter, and gestured with his cane at the closest low boulder that was only a few feet away. He didn't wait for an answer, but moved to the rock and eased himself down upon it, his legs open, his knobby knees now visible. His legs werehairy, as were his feet and toes, black hair, but at his throat wiry grey curls spilled out. His arms, on the other hand, were very white, sinewy muscle, tendons and veins visible below transparent skin that looked like sausage casing. Has he shaved his arms? Charly wondered. I bet he has, but there are long black hairs all over his fingers. Why not shave those?

The man was shifting his buttocks on the rock, getting comfortable. He looks like he's sitting on the toilet, Charly thought, suppressing a smile.

"Well, here we are, just the two of us." The man almost whispered out of the silence, and Charly suddenly felt the emptiness all around him. He glanced up the steep dune to his left, then out to the empty sea, not even a single bird there. I could run, he thought. I'd be faster. Yet he wasn't sure. And the man was interesting, and that held him in place. He performed a cascade, and a few cards fell into the sand at his feet.

"Oops," the man grinned, and Charly smiled.

"I'm just learning," he said.

"I can see that," the man said, still grinning. "And who exactly are you?"

"I'm Charly. I'm here for the festival. And who are you?"

"I'm here to see my daughter. That's who I am. Do you have a daughter?" His laugh was a cackle. "Well of course you don't."

"I have a sister, though. She's nine years old."

"Her name?" It was not a question, but a demand.

"Rosa."

He didn't seem to care.

"My daughter was Aphrodite. She still is. She was a beautiful child. Her skin was milky. Lovely blond hair. And a twinkly always." His thin eyebrows vibrated in imitation, ludicrously.

"And I would sit her down, and I would look at her when she was but a small child. And later too. Quite delicious. And, you know, I had thoughts to dress her in the raiments of a young goddess, in the way I often dressed my dolls. Have I mentioned my dolls? She was maybe fifteen then. A gown with bright stars shooting through dark fabric, meteorites, wreckage from the fiery explosion ofrockets sent up from Cape Canaveral with astronauts in them. And a halo above her lovely blond hair, there to illuminate the perfect oval of her darling face, her breasts becoming slightly prominent through that clingy fabric, though a halo is borrowed from Christians and not yet even thought of at that earlier, goddess, time. Aphrodite after all."

He had leaned his head back and seemed to be gazing up into the sky, his throat throbbing, a slight vibration in his fat cheeks. He's forgotten that I'm here, Charly thought, as he gathered his cards from the sand and set the deck on the rock beside him.

"And behind her hung a heavy tapestry, imprinted with the forms of mythic animals in various engagements such as these." He'd lowered his head and was plucking at the strange figures on his shirt, not looking at them, his eyes gazing into the air to the side of Charly's face. He doesn't even see me. A slight breeze lifted strands of his thinning hair, and his black mustache wiggled as his words spilled out. Is he about to cry? Charly thought.

"My beautiful child, Aphrodite. But, you know," he was grinning again, "when she walked out of the room, I would watch her tight little ass. It was scrumptious!" His grin fell apart, his lips then almost in a snarl.

"That's a bad word," Charly said. The man shook his head as if clearing away some sickness.

"What word?" His flinty eyes now focused on Charly's face.

"I can't say it," Charly said. "Refers to your daughter's bottom."

"Oh," the man said. "Well, anyway, let's get back to my story."

Let's? Charly thought.

Then there was silence. The man was leaning forward on his rock, seemed ready to continue. But the story had gone away, and though his mouth was open, his lips forming words, there was no sound in them. Then he smiled and finally spoke.

"What does your father do? Do you have a father?"

"He's a veterinarian," Charly said. "He cares for animals."

"Oh, my!" the man said. "I had an animal once, long ago, a capuchin monkey. He was a vicious little thing. He would press his face between the bars of his cage and glare at me and then at my dolls." The man bared his teeth in imitation of his pet, his eyes widened, his suddenly focused pupils like small black pearls. Then he shook his head and the monkey was gone. "But I haven't mentioned my dolls." He has too, Charly said to himself. "I repair these little naked figures, and I sew clothes for them. I have tiny shoes and hats too. And in my basement, these small rubbery figures are lined up as babies that have just entered the world. They are bald. There is nothing between their legs. And I imagine my monkey coming forth from his cage, in the night when I am not there. And he attacks them. Bites their heads off, tears away their arms, sinks his pointy teeth into their soft bellies. Their parts are strewn throughout the room. There is no blood, though I imagine some. It's leaking at sites of dismemberment. My monkey squats on my work table, chewing away, bits of rubber stuck between his teeth. Oh, what a jolly thought! But it wasn't real. No, no. It was only fertile imagination. I imagine things. Do you?"

"Does he have a name?" Charly asked, avoiding the man's question.

"Who?"

"Your monkey."

"Had," the man said. "He was too mean for a name. I killed him."

Charly was about to speak, to address the issue of this murder, when over the man's shoulder he saw the elephant, dancing like Dumbo, in the distance. A piñata, he thought immediately; that was easy.

It was easy because there were four balloons, on tight tether, holding the animal up above the beach and gentle surf. And it was drifting toward them, slowly, pushed along by a light breeze, growing larger.

The mid-morning sky was a deep blue, only a few wispy clouds that didn't interfere with the sun, and as the elephant approached, Charly could see the bones and organs falling in a slow tumbling shower, coming from some small opening in its belly. They formed a thin trail of anatomy in the sand.

Now, just a few hundred yards away, it had grown massive, almost to the size of one of those old time dirigibles. Charly had read about the *Hindenburg* in his studies, death, fire and destruction in a video he had seen at school. Its legs were the size of heavy logs. They swung back and forth, no more than ten feet above the beach, in shadow cast by the elephant's massive girth. Its giant saucer ears stood out rigidly from its dour head. Its trunk, like a huge anaconda, swung freely, leading it onward. It looked unfriendly, even ominous, its large vacant eyes and blunt tusks. Surely this is the biggest piñata in existence, Charly thought. How in the world did it get here. Even held up by those swollen balloons, it seemed motorized by some inexorable force within itself. Birds had been chirping in the spare growth along the dune's face, but now they were silent. The slow wash of surf at the shore line seemed to pause and become still.

The elephant hung stationary in the air for a moment, dipping to the side as if it might fall down into the sand, then righting itself. It came on then, still slowly, its belly darkening the beach behind the man's shoulders, and the tortured animal figures on his shirt came alive in its approaching shadow. Charly lowered his eyes and saw the knowing grin.

"Can you see it?" the man whispered.

How can he know? Charly thought. It's still behind him. He can't see it. Could it be some change in the atmosphere, something in the failing sun?

"Yes," he said, his voice cracking, lifting to a higher register.

"I put it there," the man said, his eyes penetrating Charly's own.

He's crazy, Charly thought, holding the man's gaze, fearful of what might happen if he looked away.

Now the elephant was moving over them, and they were in deep shadowy darkness for long moments in its passage. Thought only a few yards away, the man was now a ghost figure, some still statue, framed by the columns of the elephant's vague rear legs. The rain of organs and bones—fingers, toes, femurs, skulls—had become a flood, and Charly heard them bouncing in the sand, their spill a veil, further obscuring the man's image. When he spoke, his words seemed to come forth from a deep cave.

"Just kidding," he said. "But isn't it appropriate? The Day of the Dead after all."

Then as the elephant passed over them, and the man was visible again, Charly found he was looking across a space strewn with exotic candies and into those glittering eyes. He seemed to be expecting something, some answer to an unspoken question.

Charly reached down and lifted his deck from the rock, brushing skulls and bones aside, and performed the one hand cut without looking. He knew the huge piñata was gone down the beach behind him, but he didn't turn to follow its passage. The man was grinning, his lips moist. Then Charly spoke, his voice steady again.

"I have a story too," he said.

"Good," the man answered. "Let's hear it." He looked up and to the side, as if there was someone standing there, his daughter perhaps, and Charly began. "I was only two years old when my mother passed away. My father likes to use those words, rather than died, because he thinks that the pain he still feels is felt by me and my sister Rosa, too. She died in childbirth, and Rosa was the innocent product of her death. I've thought about this, even written those words down. There are photographs of my mother in my father's bedroom, so I know what she looked like. They were standing beside each other in one of them, both smiling, but in the other she was alone, just sitting on a porch I have never seen.

"And one day, maybe three years ago, when I was eight and a little kid and Rosa was just six years old, she stood in front of a window in our living room. She was waiting for our father to come home from work, but she was facing me, acting like she wasn't waiting. I was working at the coffee table. I'd spread a beach towel, like this one, over it, so I wouldn't scratch it with my magic kit. I was doing one of the scarf tricks, and I couldn't get it, so I wasn't looking at her, though I could feel her being there. Then, after a while, she coughed and shuffled her feet on the carpet, and I looked up.

"The sun was bright in the window behind her, and
at first she was only a shadow standing there. I had
to squint against the glare. Then, all of a sudden, I
saw the figure behind her. It was my mother. I knew
her from the pictures. She was dressed in a gown that
seems to me now a little like the one you said your
daughter wore, but the figures on her dress were not
celestial in that way. They were flowers, coreopsis
and daylilies. I'd studied up on the flowers around
our house, so I knew their names.

"I thought, 'my mother,' and it was then that she
became smaller and smaller, until she was finally just
the outline of her body, there, behind Rosa, just as if
she had melted into her. Rosa. My mother's face was
her face. I had never seen that. My mother. I didn't
remember her, but she seemed alive again now in my
sister.

"Then Rosa heard the car in the drive and ran from
the window to the door. Our father was home. I think
I remember that I cried a little then. I didn't know
why, but I do now."

Charly felt moisture in his eyes and blinked it away.
Then he focused on the man's face again. No longer was he smiling that cruel smile. His cheeks had
sagged slightly, and he looked older and troubled,
seemed to be searching his tortured mind for some
sort of explanation, momentarily bewildered in the
conventional, simple beauty of Charly's story.

How could a child become a mother? It was her child. Had the amniotic fluids somehow imprinted her image in the skin of her daughter, an identity passed on at some point on the brink of impending death? I can see it, photographs and genes and lips and fingernail clippings floating in the fluids, all being sucked, as if down a drain, into the fallopian tube, then in through the navel of the unborn child.

All this was said aloud, though the man seemed sure he was only thinking it. His hairy hands were moving in the air near his face as he articulated his thoughts.

Then, for a moment, considering the image of the child and mother and Charly's tears, something edged its way between the dark layered slabs of madness deep within him. It was a mild, subdued light, the light of conventional sanity, and it was calm and as beautiful as the sand under his feet and the hard, still, rock on which he sat. And it was frightening, and he struggled to pull himself away from it.

Charly saw his face relax, his eyes become clear and focused, but only for a moment. Then that face that was like a carnival mask took shape once again, and the man was nodding his head, up and down, up and down, flecks of spittle dripping from the corners of his mouth. He wiped the spit away with his hairy hand and returned to the person he had always been.

"A very nice story," he said. "Did you make it up? Of course you did."

Charly didn't respond.

"Well," the man said. "I must be going," and he pushed his cane into the sand and struggled to his feet. He said nothing more. He just turned and made his way slowly down to the surf line where the sand was spare and hardened, then moved along the beach, heading back toward the town and the ongoing commotion of the Day of the Dead celebration.

Charly watched him as he grew smaller. Then he picked up his deck of cards and his blanket and towel and made his way back to the Sea Burst. I will tell no one, he thought, not my father and not Edna Hobby. I will keep this to myself.

CHAPTER 12

APHRODITE, 5:00 pm

For the sake of some drama, I have not mentioned my father's letter, not the one he left for me at the house so many years ago, but the one that was delivered to the post office last week. Nor have I mentioned the fabric label I cut from my father's shirt, that one you'll remember I took from our house before leaving. The label is now tucked among those autopsy papers in Ram Chopra's apartment. I put it there a few days ago, on my last round trip. Entry was quite simple. Ram was out to dinner, maybe with Angie, and the lock was child's play. I've been waiting, but the good doctor has now taken up with Lisa James, and his searches among the papers have been put on hold for the time being. Lisa, as writers often say, which is the case with any character, seems to be taking on a life of her own. It might be sex, or fascination, or merely inquisitiveness. I cannot say. All these people that I have created are beginning to move on, to move away from my control. Only my father has been real.

As the sun begins its slow decline into the distant west, maybe a cowboy movie voice-over should have said that, I'm still a few hours from my destination and nightfall. There is no breeze to speak of, nor has the day cooled down significantly, good news for the revelers. I've eaten my sandwich and drunk my water, and now, even as I tire a bit, my backpack is lighter, and I have enough energy to keep up my pace. Traffic, but not much.

Once the letter was in my hands and I'd mulled over it for a while, I opened the folder I'd taken from my father's torture room and looked through it in earnest. I'd never had the stomach for this study, nor did I want to disabuse myself of thinking of my father at least as a victim—the diabetes and its complications—in his own right. Now I had to put that yearned for judgment aside and return to the real world.

At least there were no photographs in the folder, only my father's careful renderings of women undergoing what I hoped were imagined tortures. These were difficult enough to gaze upon, but what ended up as a more terrifying possibility were the notes and among them the carefully penned-in names. There were four of them, and after a few phone calls I learned that three of these women had gone missing many years ago, at least a year or so before my father's supposed suicide. Missing was one thing. There was at least some hope in it. But the fourth woman, one Inder Chopra, had been found in a car in a junkyard, tortured and killed, though not raped. I considered then that all four were my father's victims. That seemed an inescapable conclusion, though I had a wish to deny it, which lasted only a few days, until I began to think about justice. No need to go through it again. Betrayal after betrayal.

After a few more phone calls, I discovered that Inder's husband was a medical doctor, this Ram Chopra, and that he now resided in the very town I was heading for, in the clinic where I have placed him. This may seem an unreasonable coincidence (and there is one more to follow and that at the end of my father's letter), but then I'm telling the story, and so it goes.

Here's the letter.

My Dear Aphrodite,

You'll be amazed and possibly troubled to hear from me now. *I guess so!*

I've been away for years, it's true, but it seems I'm still among the living, and I write in the hopes that you'll forgive my big deception and agree to spend some time with me. I'll come to you. In fact, I have come. You can find me in this town at the foot of the peninsula. I have learned that you visit here from time to time, and I hope you'll see fit to visit with me. Dinner? Maybe some relaxing time on the beach? Whatever you'd like, my dear daughter.

You can reach me through the desk at this place called the Sea Burst. Just ask for Gregory Hephaestus, the name I go by now.

Your Loving Father

Ah, well. Once again the insane matter of factness of his words. Had nothing happened? I guess not in his eyes. I didn't respond. Then in awhile I thought better of that, and responded coolly, giving an uncertain date for my arrival. I'd decided I wanted to keep him there, at least long enough. I had plans for him, and I set out in the ensuing days to execute them.

CHAPTER 13

WEDNESDAY

MONDAY HAD SEEN A CACOPHONY OF NOISE AND activity, frantic and experimental, as celebrants worked to get themselves situated. The town itself had seemed to vibrate, children and adults in half-costume, long, circuitous lines at amusement park rides and beach blankets and coolers flooded by the incoming tide. Drunkards roamed the streets, some collapsing onto passing family members, and a few awkward fights broke out, the young summer police hires having a devil of a timekeeping even a bit of order. The mayor was up late, as was Ram Chopra, contusions and superficial cuts to be tended to as well as a couple of heat exhaustion patients. There were only a few animal casualties, that sheep, a dog, and an injured raccoon that had wandered onto main street, bewildered, then had been kicked to the curb by a father who feared for his children, this resulting in a broken leg that was set and soft-casted by Ernesto Olivares, the animal then given a quiet place to heal.

By mid-day Tuesday, things were close to being routinized. Weekly tickets to ride at the amusement park had been sold to those families that had formerly stood in hot sun in long lines. New piñatas had been floated over the beach, replacing those that, in an unorderly frenzy, had been whacked into submission, their anatomical candies, femurs, finger bones, small skulls, and a variety of internal organs, flooding down into the sand, and all who wished for them had acquired their full costumes in the shops along main street and from the vendors perambulating along the streets and beach. The drunks remained drunk, the bars raucous and full, but they now caused few injuries, neither human nor animal, and the medical clinic was enjoying, for the time being at least, quiet times.

Ernesto and Charly had visited the amusement park in the late afternoon, Ernesto full of enthusiasm for time spent with his son, though Charly was subdued. "Something on your mind?" Ernesto asked. "Just a little tired," Charly replied, but he awakened to his father's laughter as they took on a half dozen rides, poking each other on their shoulders as they looked down at some mariachi musicians who danced as they played their instruments below them as they rode to the top of the Ferris wheel. After that, they dined on tamales and refried beans, purchased from a food cart, topped off by Cokes and a few hip bones and small, articulate, skulls. Charly had told his father about the nice lady he had met on the beach, but not about the man, and though Ernesto had questioned him about her, he hadn't pushed the issue. The two had returned to the Sea Burst early and phoned the camp to speak briefly with Rosa. She said she had much to tell, what fun!, but she couldn't talk for very long because they were making lanyards! She had to gather with the other kids. "A very good day, indeed!" Ernesto had said, and Charly emphatically agreed.

Tuesday night, and Lisa James and her mother, Edna Hobby, sat at a table in the bar together, listening to Bo Bogardus tickle the ivories with some quiet jazz ballads, *My Old Flame, The Shadow of Your Smile*. The hotel was off the beaten path, and while the bar was full of patrons in Day of the Dead clothing, conversations were no more than a dull drone, light laughter and pleasant talk, the scene as subdued as the music. And Edna was smiling, listening to her daughter, who spoke a bit mysteriously of this man she had met. "His name is Ram. An odd name, but he's softer than that. It's very soon, but I think there may be a future here."

She couldn't get over her mother's interest in her interest, her soothing words. What has happened to her? Edna glanced up as Angelo Camp entered the room. They smiled at each other. Then he was gone, into the kitchen, the laundry, the halls, his office, behind the front desk. He was trying to push the evening along. He'd be seeing Ram for dinner tomorrow night, at which time he'd tell his story.

Ram, for his part, was sitting at his desk, thinking about Lisa James. He'd be seeing her for lunch tomorrow. He shook his head. Quit mooning, he thought, and reached for the autopsy folder, still in his romantic daze, and knocked it off the desk onto the floor. A piece of fabric peeked out from among the spilled pages. What is that? He thought.

At which point Ned Hobby stepped into the bar and made his way over to the piano. He was carrying a sketch pad, a few pencils sticking up from his shirt pocket. He found room at a table just a few feet from Bo, who glanced up from the keys and smiled warmly at him. Ned's face was flushed, as he removed one of the pencils and began to sketch.

And in the far corner of the room, a rather stout man in dark glasses, dressed a little too formally, sat alone at a table, a gin and tonic in his thick fingered hand, a cane propped against the empty chair across from him. He may have been gazing at Lisa and Edna, but it was hard to tell. His glasses protected his vision from any intrusion. Perhaps he was thinking of something, perhaps not.

Wednesday evening. They decided they would dine at a casino a few miles from the town. The place was known for its good food, in a restaurant a good distance from the gaming tables. It might be crowded, but it was at least away from the town, and both needed relief from the churning celebration. Ram drove and thought about the label and his day's investigations, and Angie worried about his problems.

Ram couldn't imagine how he had missed it. He'd been through the papers dozens of times. Had it stuck to the back of one of them? That didn't seem likely. But there it was.

He lifted it from the floor and smoothed it out on his desk. It was a label, cut from inside the collar of a shirt, or from the edge of the tail: the name of a manufacturer and below that what looked like a store's name, followed by the name of a town in Wisconsin. He lifted the phone and called long distance information, then he called the number that was given.

"Oh, ya. That was special order, oh boy, a long time ago. Maybe out of business now. I can try 'em maybe."

"Many buyers? Can you remember?"

"Ya, for sure. Just the one though."

"Just one?"

"Special order, ya know, just the one."

"Can you tell me the name?"

"Oh, ya. No problem there. Some kind of a sad story, though. Sure."

"So?" Ram said. "What's the story?"

"Well, he drowned in the Big Winny. Years ago it was. It seems he must have drowned."

"What is that?"

"What's what?"

"The Big Winny."

"Oh, that! It's lake Winnebago, sir. Biggest lake up here. She's thirty miles long, 'bout ten wide. That's big as Cuba, ya know. Well, at least as long. She's a big one."

"I know of that," Ram said.

"What?"

"Winnebago. I know of that."

"Ah," the man said. "Well, the police found his clothing on the beach there. Decided it was suicide. Never did find his body."

"Do you have a name?"

"Oh, ya, sure. It's Oscar Hermanson."

"Do you know where he lived?"

"Who?"

"This Hermanson."

"Well, gee-whiz. I live right here. Above the store."

"No, no. I mean the man who drowned."

"Oh, that one! Appell, it was. Rodney Appell. But his house is sold now. Long gone. There was a daughter, ya, but she's long gone too, far as I know."

"Can you tell me what he looked like? This Appell guy."

"Oh, sure. He was a pudgy kinda guy, thinning on the head. He fixed dolls. Even built some."

"His profession?"

"Sure was."

"And his daughter? Anything about her."

"Well, she walked a lot. All over the town. Moved east, as I heard. Onto some peninsular or other. Must have liked being close to water."

"Do you know the state?"

"Of her health? No, I don't know that."

"No. The state she moved to."

"No, I don't know that. It was out east. All I know."

"Okay." Ram said. "Thank you very much."

"What about the shirt? Do ya want me ta try and get one?"

"No. Thank you. For the information I mean."

"Well, okay. Thanks for calling then."

"Right," Ram said, and then he hung up.

A peninsula, he thought. Could it be this one? He felt the edge of rage rise up into his temples. Then he turned the label over, and there penned in neatly on the back was a name, Gregory Hephaestus, followed by another name, Sea Burst.

They sat at a table off in the corner of the casino dining room, a couple of martinis on the crisp white cloth in front of them, and Angelo told him about his gambling and the trouble he found himself in. He was shy and somewhat embarrassed in the telling, but when Ram questioned him in his quiet, accepting voice, Angie relaxed a little.

"How much do you owe?" Ram asked.

"A little over thirty thousand. But with the vig, that gets bigger every week."

"And will you continue?"

"With the gambling? No way in hell," Angie said. "Absolutely not."

"And the drugs? What about that?"

"They really aren't connected. That's for sex only."

"I didn't think so."

"So what do you think I should do?" Angie asked, shy once again, feeling like a child.

"I think you shouldn't worry," Ram said. "It'll all be okay."

They'd moved their drinks to the side to make room for the pasta dishes the waiter delivered, and Ram was digging in, while Angelo looked across the room, wondering just why he shouldn't worry. Then a shadow fell across their table, and the hand of a large, bulky man, banged down on the cloth beside Angie's plate, his martini glass falling over and spilling its contents onto the floor. Other patrons, hearing the sound, glanced over, then looked away. They both looked up at him. He was grinning, his thick lips moist. Dark, milky eyes staring hard at Angie.

"Tomorrow," he said. "That's your day. You damn well better be on time. There are no more days left."

Angie started to speak. Then Ram reached across the table and grabbed the man's thick wrist, holding his hand down where it was.

The man looked across at him in surprise, lurched back a little, but Ram held his hand in place. Then he growled and struck out with his fist, aiming for Ram's face. Ram caught the punch in his palm and held fast, and the man began to struggle, dancing in place, both hands trapped in Ram's grip.

"What the fuck are you doing?" he hissed, still struggling, and Ram spoke quietly to him.

"Relax," he said. "The money is forthcoming. Right now. Can you relax?"

"Yeah," the man said. "Okay." He quit fighting, and Ram released him and reached into his jacket for his checkbook.

"How much exactly?" he asked.

"Thirty, plus six," the man said.

Ram wrote the check, then reached out to hand it to him. The man hesitated.

"Take it," Ram said. "It's good. Now get out of here."

He took it, slipped it into his pocket, and turned and left, feeling the eyes of other diners as he walked across the room.

Angie was dumbfounded.

"You can't," he said. "That's a lot of money. And that guy, how did you do that to him?"

"First of all, I can," Ram said. "I'm rich. I've told you that. The money is of no importance. And besides that, you're my friend. As to the rest, it was a kind of mind over matter. Something learned as a child in India. Doctor Mysterioso." He was smiling. Then they were both laughing, and when they'd finished their meal, Angelo insisted on picking up the check.

It was on the way back when Ram asked him if there might be someone in his hotel named Hephaestus, and Angie said he'd check.

When Ned rose from Bo's bed, he was a little shaky on his pins, and Bo turned over onto his side. Wow, he thought.

The room was very much the same as his own, though a little smaller and on a lower floor. The same mahogany and glass, the same well-appointed bathroom. He showered and dressed, then went back into the bedroom, took up his sketch pad and began to draw. The figure of Bo in the bed, his face in sleeping profile.

What in the world, Ned thought. All these years with women, and this is what I've wanted. He knew, or at least suspected, that it would be a temporary thing. He didn't care. They would go out and eat together. They would spend time on the beach. Maybe more time in bed. He felt a quiet turmoil in his groin at the thought. All these years. He looked at his half-completed drawing. It was good, very good, he thought. Next would come the painting. He wanted to tell someone. Not his mother. That's for sure. Maybe Lisa. Though he had only just met her, he thought she might understand. He would draw men to begin with. Then he would paint their figures.

He thought of his childhood, his time in the Navy and his tenure in art school. Had it been there then? Even thinking back, he could identify nothing. Yet he knew he had remained a child, even when he had consorted with women, those who had treated him as a child, as had his mother, even until the last few days. He didn't feel like one anymore. He felt like a man, or at least he felt like a different person. Fifty-three years old. Imagine that. And only now an adult.

He moved to the bed and reached down and stroked Bo's cheek, and as he awakened he whispered, "Turn your head." Then he returned to his chair by the window and started a new drawing. Later, he thought, out on the beach, I'll drawn him there. Then we'll go swimming. Then we'll have a little lunch.

That one across the room, he thought. She looks like Aphrodite. Blonde hair at least, and the figure I remember. That might be interesting. My dear child, Aphrodite. Your rosy cheeks, perky little breasts when you were but a child. I'd have dressed you in gowns I'd sewn for my dolls, after first applying your underwear and jabbing you gently with those sharp little pins, small tight buttocks and hips I used in my careful constructions, your skin as smooth and rubbery as my miniature children. There would have been more, and more. I'd have preserved you and protected you, safe as the ones on the mantle. The blood pumped through his arms and legs and behind his failing eyes at the thought of this and the darker thoughts of the woman sitting beside the older one across the room. There will be no negotiations. No answer for the pleadings. Just his pure pleasure.

He had seen this woman entering the medical clinic just two days ago. She'd stayed in there longer than seemed necessary, and when she'd left, the doctor had touched her intimately on the shoulder at the door. She'd seemed flushed, and he had followed her back to the hotel before quitting his observations. After only a few minutes of thought, he had a plan.

He had been staying at the hotel for more than a week, waiting for his daughter's arrival, but she had not come. He was waiting, and he walked the town beach, drank sweet liqueurs in the bars, ate sparingly at various restaurants. Then had come the first days of the Day of the Dead festival. He liked the name, and he roamed the streets among costumed revelers, ate cotton candy and those small bones that were like the ones he imagined beneath the smooth tight skin of his dolls. He walked the rise of the dunes, and at some point discovered the hut perched on the crest like the turret of some half-ruined castle of old, the place where Rapunzel had been held captive. He forced the lock easily, and on another trip replaced it with his own. He entered the hut, cleaned it, and prepared his nest. It was like one, designed for the housing of fledgling birds, little children, dolls, and even childlike women. That one, he thought, once again gazing at the blonde across the room. A trail of crumbs? He'd figure the lure. Tomorrow, he thought, in the clear light of day.

How soon do we age and come closer to death. His eyes, those most important instruments, had been failing for years, though he could still see, just enough for capturing the images, and now, after all these years, the living figures those images held. Finally, he will see them both, this woman as well as his beloved daughter. He lifted his cane and tapped the rubber tip on his toes. Then he pressed down hard, enjoying the pain that awakened his lust. No, it really isn't lust, but he had no other term for it. My dear Aphrodite, have you guessed at the name. Hephaestus, husband of the goddess herself? Just an indulgence on his part, something quite harmless, a joke even.

The intervening years had seen him as a consultant to small doll factories, mostly in the West, California and Oregon, matters of costuming and mold-making, never making use of the cachet of his real name. At each place he had to prove himself, and he had managed to do so quickly. The money was good enough to keep him going, though he knew he was going nowhere, certainly not where he needed to go. Now he was here. Now he would gather what was left of his family. Just the two of them, together once again.

He looked across at the young woman, her hair and smooth skin. Though his wish was for his daughter, his dear Aphrodite, he now hoped there would be time for this other. That return to pleasure. What had been held back for so long a time.

It was getting late. The hotel barroom was beginning to empty. He saw a man pass through quickly, then leave to go elsewhere. He thought it might be the owner or manager. Another man sat close to the piano, drawing a likeness of the player, a clear intensity in his gaze. Tomorrow, Thursday, he was thinking, knowing he would have to work things out. The sounds of the festival doings had faded to a quiet murmur in the far distance. He sipped his drink, then drained the glass down to the wedge of lime. Then he lifted his cane again and struggled to his feet, feeling a little stiff. Once he'd adjusted his spine and pulled himself erect, he strolled carefully across the small dance floor, heading for his room. The piano player, a dark handsome young man, was playing show tunes. He listened to the strains of something familiar as he left the room. *Someday My Prince Will Come.*

CHAPTER 14

THURSDAY

SHE WOKE EARLY IN THE MORNING, after fitful sleep. Already she was anticipating lunch with him. It was only six am. What should I wear? Something subdued? Something sexy? She went into the bathroom and took a long hot shower, then she dried and brushed out her hair and dressed for the day. She was to meet her mother, Edna, downstairs for breakfast in the hotel at 7:00 am. I might change clothes for lunch. Then she gathered her rolls of film and put them in her purse. She'd drop them off at the pharmacy for developing before heading to the restaurant and Ram. Later, in her darkroom at home, she'd see what she had. He really is something special. Am I kidding myself? In his bed above the clinic, after the loving, he had told her of the death of his wife, years ago, and she, with no guarding awareness, had spilled out her own story, her husband's infidelity, the accidental murder, the trial. He had accepted it all without judgment, only quiet, soothing words. What a man, she thought. A beautiful man.

It was almost 7:00 am, and when she went to the door to descend for breakfast, she found the envelope on the floor near the sill. She lifted it and went to the upholstered chair near the window and opened it. It contained a letter written in fine, somewhat feminine script, the signature, Ram, penned in at the bottom. She read it, then read it again.

> *My Dear Woman Lisa,*
>
> *May I call you Aphrodite, Goddess of Love? I have a surprise for you. Would you come and meet me at 10:00 this morning? I'll leave a trail for you. And below are a few directions. It will be fun! I look forward to seeing you there.*
>
> *Your admirer,*
>
> *Ram*

My God, she thought, what an odd, formal letter, yet she felt a distinct tingling in her loins. Of course I'll come, she said to his signature, then she read through the letter and the directions once again.

Edna was waiting at the table when she arrived, and she smiled her new smile as Lisa sat down.

"Breakfast," she said, "But I can tell you're already thinking of lunch."

Lisa laughed. "You've got me there, Mother."

They both laughed.

Just cereal with banana and strawberries, then cups of coffee. They ate slowly, talking all through the meal.

What do you think of your brother? And you, what do you think of your son? And photography. And this doctor. This boy you met on the beach. The erstwhile husband, not spoken of. Will you stay through Sunday? How long will *you* stay? Animated conversation. All smiles. Her mother would meet the boy later. They'd go for a few rides in the amusement park. Then they'd go swimming. And Lisa would change again, then head out for the place outlined in Ram's directions. She didn't speak of her 10:00 am meeting, feeling it was private, a kind of secret liaison. But first she'd drop off the rolls of film.

The sandy path that led through the dunes was edged with beach grass, rugosa roses and low growth dusty miller. She wore sandals, and the sand flowed between her toes as she made her way. The path rose slowly until she was almost climbing, and when she looked down and her feet reached hard ground, she saw the marzipan finger bones, small skulls, and what looked like doll parts, tiny hands and feet. They had been cast alongside and in her path every few yards. She couldn't imagine why they were there. Could this be part of Ram's surprise? How could it be? Then, nearing the top where the ground leveled and high growth to both sides created a kind of tunnel, she saw the roof of the hut, then the whole small structure at the cliff's edge and to her right the beach and the sea below.

The door was only a few feet from the cliff, and when she knocked she heard a faint shuffling from inside.

"Ram?" she called out tentatively, but there was no answer. Then the door opened upon a man in dark glasses.

"Where's Ram?" she said.

"Soon, soon," he said. "Welcome. Do come in."

She entered, and the door was locked behind her.

Ned and Bo decided to spend the day at the beach. For Bo it was a lark, at least so far it was, though he was already beginning to wonder. For Ned it was more than that. It was a beginning. As a nod to the festival, Bo had purchased a pair of skull bathing caps, ones that depicted brains, as if the actual skull had been sawed away to reveal them. Otherwise they wore swimsuits and skeleton T-shirts, matching ones, but of different colors: red for Ned that matched his blushing, black for Bo, who was the darker of the two. They walked the streets holding hands, their passage for Ned like striding through a gauntlet. There were many gay couples in the town, though none in evidence just then, and they heard twitters of light laughter. Ned was sure people were laughing at them, but Bo squeezed his hand, knowing better. It's just the usual frivolity, he thought. But if it was more than that, he didn't much care.

They carried towels and beach chairs provided by the hotel and lunch sandwiches and drinks purchased at a deli in town. Though Ned was the elder, he was the novice in this situation, and it was Bo who directed their progress.

Once they were set up on the beach near the surf line, Bo insisted on rubbing lotion into Ned's shoulders and back, and when he said "Now do me," Ned complied, though he looked around to make sure no one was watching before doing so. Bo registered his hesitancy.

"Look," he said softly and warmly. "This is the way of it. These simple things."

He was beginning to feel more than he wanted to, and he liked that feeling.

They entered the quiet surf side by side, both a little flushed from the sun. The water was pleasantly cool under a sky holding a few wispy clouds. There were a few small boats in the distance, the sounds of Day of the Dead celebrants coming across the water, Mexican music and singing, and they stood chest deep in the sea looking out at them. Bo was feeling frisky and would have liked to wrestle a little in the water, but he restrained himself in honor of Ned's newness in this situation. This is something else, he thought. He's never felt like this, and maybe neither have I. He'd off-loaded some drugs to Angelo Camp at the hotel, but since he'd met Ned he'd forgotten about such business.

They ate their lunch sitting beside each other in their chairs, their brains close together. And they spoke of their past lives, sharing their stories in complete honesty. Ned told him of his current concern about his art, and Bo confessed his desire to end the drug business and get serious about his piano playing.

"I like your playing," Ned said, and Bo said he liked Ned's drawings.

"Not because they're of *me*!" he said, and they both laughed.

People gathered on the beach came and went, and in the early afternoon Ned spied his mother and a young boy playing some game or other, or something like a game, on a blanket not far away. He caught her eye, and she waved at him, wiggling her fingers and smiling. He couldn't imagine what had gotten into her. Something, that's for sure.

"Do you like shellfish?" Bo asked.

"Sure. All of it," Ned replied.

"Well, I know of a place. Excellent lobster, steamers and clams. It's a casual shack, just a short walk from our hotel."

"Sounds good," Ned said.

"Once we get back, we can shower and dress, then go there for dinner, my treat."

"No. Mine."

"I insist," Bo said.

"So do I," Ned said, and they both laughed.

Ned leaned over and kissed Bo on the mouth, fleetingly, without care, and Bo was warmed by such casual gesture. He was getting there, he thought. And, by God, so am I!

When they got back to Ned's room at the hotel, they fell into each other's arms.

Dinner can wait.

Lisa didn't show up for lunch, and Ram couldn't understand why. Had he said something, done something?No, that couldn't be it. Something must have come up, maybe something important. He called the hotel from the restaurant, but she wasn't in. Then he called her mother, but she too was out, so he picked up a sandwich at one of the vending carts and headed back to the clinic, where he found there were people waiting, cuts and bruises, and one serious stomach problem.

He worked through the day, taking time out to call once more. She was still not there. Again he called her mother, but she hadn't seen Lisa, didn't know where she was. At day's end, after calling Angie to make sure things were okay and to check on this Gregory Hephaestus—he was indeed a resident at the Sea Burst—he went out to eat with Ernesto and his son Charly, a bright sweet kid. They went to a seafood shack just a few blocks from their hotel. They were also staying at Angie's place.

A handsome gay couple sat at a table near them in quiet conversation. Both Ernesto and Ram recognized them, wondering about their recent history. The place was full, but subdued, and though Ram was somewhat preoccupied with concerns for Lisa, he listened to Charly's innocent talk about magic and magnets, and he and Ernesto spoke for a time about medicine, what their day had brought them, people and animals. They finished dinner, all eating a fine fish chowder, as the sun was sinking. It was getting close to 8:00, and Ram walked the father and son back to the Sea Burst, then decided that he needed more walking, and headed down to the beach beyond the amusement park where he and Angie often met. He took his shoes off and tucked them under the boards, then set out toward the surf. Lisa was on his mind, but so was Gregory Hephaestus, who by evidence of the shirt label he now believed was the murderer of his wife. Rage rose in him at the thought, but it was strangely softened by his desire for Lisa, a woman he had just met. His rage had now turned to conviction and retribution and resolve.

Fires burned on the beach, and he could see shadowy figures and marshmallows glimmering at the end of long sticks in the flames. A few people splashed at the ocean's edge, and there was singing and instruments and the creak of metal at the amusement park in the distance. A few rockets rose, then fizzled out over the surf. It goes on, he thought. But only for three more days. He'd be glad when it was over, but maybe not so glad if Lisa was no longer there. He could see a future, tentatively, with her.

He headed off into the darkness away from the town and its turmoil, down the beach toward where those boulders cut across it on their way into the sea. Not too long a walk, but a refreshing one. A light breeze ruffled his hair, then went away as the dunes rose up into cliffs. There was no moon, but a bright starry sky lit his way. No one, just the quiet wash of the incoming tide. Then he reached the turning, and the distant sounds of revelry drifted away. He could see the dark shapes of the boulders in the far distance. I'll turn around when I get there and head back, he thought. Then, when I get back home, I'll call the hotel again, or maybe I'll just walk there, get a drink, listen to that piano player.

When he reached the boulders, now massive and distinct in starlight, he sat down on one of them and considered things, and it was when he was troubling the disappearance of Lisa yet again that he looked up and saw faint light coming from above. What is that? he thought.

He got up and moved toward the sea until his bare feet were in the surf and saw the flickering more clearly. That's coming from the hut, he thought. Must be an oil lamp or something battery powered. It doesn't make sense this time of night, or any night. Could be kids or some of these Day of the Dead revelers. He didn't like it, and he decided to go up there and see what was going on. So he walked back to the boardwalk, fetched his shoes from under it, and set out on the dune path heading for the high crest.

The breeze rose into a light wind as he ascended, and when he reached the high growth near the top, tall grasses brushed against his shoulders and arms. Then he approached the hut door, keeping well away from the cliff's edge that seemed closer in the darkness.

He knocked on the door, somewhat tentatively. Nothing. So he knocked again, more firmly this time. He heard a shuffling inside, the slide of what he took to be a piece of furniture, then a muffled woman's scream. Lisa, he thought, and though he was not sure that it was she, he stepped back and kicked hard at the place above the handle. It didn't budge, so he stepped back, then rushed forward and banged into the door's edge with his shoulder. Again nothing. He was getting pissed. This was not a sturdy building, though it was carefully constructed and true on its foundation. He edged his way back to the darkness at the cliff's edge. He could feel the breeze in his cuffs as it rose up from the beach far below, and he leaned forward and charged at the door with all the speed and force he could muster. He hit it hard with his shoulder, feeling the pain, then bounced off it and fell back toward the cliff, almost going over. He was on his back now, his head and shoulders out in the empty air. He struggled carefully to his feet and crossed to the door and felt along its surface where his fingers found not the place of the dead bolt, but some sort of emblem above it. This is where I've kicked it, he thought. The correct place is lower. So again he stepped away, breathed deeply, now hearing no voices or activity from within, and kicked out at the right place, feeling a sharp pain through the heel of his tennis shoes. This time it gave, a crack of wood and the scrape of metal, and the door flew open, banged against the inside wall, then flew back at him as he stepped over the sill, hitting him full in the face and knocking him to the floor of the hut. He rose slowly, his wind gone and his vision hazy, and tasted the blood that was dripping from his nose down to his lips. He wiped it away with his sleeve, his eyes blinking, struggling to focus in the dimly illuminated darkness.

He could see the glow of the oil lamp off on a table in the corner and the shadow of the figure seated in a chair at the far wall. There were other dim objects in his way, and he was careful of them as he made his way to the lamp, reached down and raised the wick. Then the room's contents became visible.

Photographs of a young woman and a girl who had become this woman dressed every wall, and in the spaces between them, naked doll figures had been nailed up through various parts of their small vulnerable bodies with what looked like steak knives. He saw one attached with a knife thrust through her soft belly, another pinned there through her vacant eye. Above the glow of the oil lamp hung a dress that had been finely sewn with star and meteor figures, a sky full of them. It was hung on a hanger, and it rippled slightly in the light breeze that now came in through the open door. There were renderings too, drawings not of dolls, but of carefully depicted women in erotic poses, tears on their cheeks, mouths open in silent screams.

"My Goodness! You didn't have to knock the door down. I was coming."

But he had not been coming. He was lounging in a kitchen chair at the far wall, and his voice, though pitched in a high register, was oily and smooth and seemingly without care.

"Come in," he said. "Now that you *are* in. Welcome."

He wore a blue, short sleeved seersucker shirt, buttoned at the collar where a leathery black bow tie, like those usually worn with tuxedos, had been attached.

His pants were khaki cargo shorts, and his spindly legs were crossed at the knees, his foot, encased in a leather work boot that seemed too heavy for that small foot, dangled down, swinging a little in the air. His arms were smooth, but Ram could see the thick hair on his hands, one on his knee, the other close to his crotch. His cheeks seemed slightly swollen, his lips livery. Though his belly was fat, he seemed to be wasting away. Thin, wiry arms, folds of flesh hanging at his neck. But his eyes, though hazy, held the dark glow of black onyx, his pupils bright pinpoints of golden light. Beside the dress and behind him hung a long rubber apron of the kind worn by technicians in x-ray or doctors in autopsy.

Ram turned slowly away from him, tentatively, afraid of what he might find. And there was Lisa.

She was tied to a straight back chair, her wrists strapped to the arms and her ankles secured to the chair's front legs with duct tape. A rag dangled from her mouth, held in place by a thick rubber band circling her head, holding her fine blonde hair close to her scalp. She was naked and quaking, her eyes pleading, and Ram vowed not to look at her body as he approached her. This endeavor failed, but she didn't seem to notice as he stared at her lovely breasts and the small moon curve of her stomach. He pulled the band free and watched her hair fall and fan out, disheveled, as after sex. It licked at her bare shoulders. She spit out the rag, looked up at him and spoke.

"It's about time," she said. "That was one hell of a whack you took at the door there." Then she smiled. There were tears flooding down her cheeks, and she had begun to laugh and couldn't stop, her laughter lifting up almost into hysteria.

Ram glanced at the man. He was still sitting there. Then he placed his hands on Lisa's naked shoulders and spoke quietly to her.

"It's okay now," he said.

Then he loosened her bonds. She rubbed at her wrists, then, almost sheepishly, reached down to the purse that rested on the floor at the chair's side and fished out her Djarum cigarettesand a lighter.

"What took you so long?" She asked. "I was getting impatient."

"Dinner," he said. "With the vet and his son. I lost track of time. The boy told a joke."

"Let's hear it."

"Okay. What do a lemon and a chicken have in common."

"And?"

"They're both yellow. Except for the chicken."

She laughed, then shuddered. How could they be saying these things, talking and joking, while all the while he sits there, waiting? She'd wanted to be elsewhere, someplace wholesome, but she wasn't.

"Go ahead, Ram said. "Smoke. It's over. Just give me a few moments." He touched her cheek, caressed it with his fingers, then turned and crossed the room to where the man still sat, seemingly relaxed, though he held a cane now and was tapping its tip on the floor.

"You're Hephaestus, aren't you?" Ram said, asking a question that was not one.

"Well, yes," the man said, matter-of-factly, grinning up at him. "I am. For the time being at least. And who are you?"

"I'm death," Ram said. "You killed my wife."

"Oh, well. I don't know about that. Which one was she?"

His rubber bow tie shook under his chin. He was laughing silently at what he took to be his joke. He wiggled his cane, and Ram reached out and pulled it away from him and threw it away.

"I'll need that, you know." Hephaestus said.

"Not anymore," Ram answered.

Then the man tilted his head to the side, his mustache twitching, his mouth in an expression of concern.

"You don't understand," he said. "Everything is alright here."

Then Ram moved closer, and the man uncrossed his legs and opened them to let the other in. Ram fell to his knees in front of him, his thighs pressed against the chair's seat, and reached out and placed his hands around the man's neck, just under his tie, and began to squeeze. The tie wiggled as his Adam's apple lifted, then it fell away, bouncing on the floor beside the chair.

Ram was taller than the man, but on his knees, he had to reach up and extend his arms as he applied pressure.

Cigarette ashes fell to Lisa's naked breasts. She could have dressed herself. Her clothes had been neatly folded and placed on the metal table that held the man's instruments. But she couldn't move. The activities at the end of the room held her in thrall. She could hear that Ram was speaking, constantly, but she couldn't get his words, there where he knelt like a supplicant reaching up in prayer to lift an icon, which was the man's head, his face beginning to glow, a dark red rising in his cheeks. Even his eyes, though clearly attempting to focus on Ram's face below him, seemed ready to bleed.

It took a long time, Ram whispering up into the man's face, the man grabbing at Ram's arms, that heavy charm bracelet clanking at his wrist, vibrating and shaking, his head lurching from side to side. And he was attempting to speak as well, to answer something that Ram was asking, his fat, dark lips forming words, the silent, choking contents of which could not be ascertained, though their tone was apparent in his mouth and undulating cheeks. Was he smiling, laughing, explaining? Lisa wasn't sure. But he was clearly engaged in the conversation that would soon end in his extinction. Then he was drooling, a foamy moisture erupting at the corners of his mouth, then falling to bathe Ram's fingers as they flexed and tightened at his throat, thumbs pressing into his windpipe. It's almost over, Lisa thought.

Then his head began to fall, and soon his chin was resting on those tightening fingers. His hands, which near the end had been weakly caressing Ram's shoulders and arms like a lover, slipped down to hang at his sides. Ram released him then, and gripping his spread knees, pushed himself up to his feet. The man still sat in the chair. There was no movement in him. He might have been sleeping, but Lisa could tell that he was dead. And suddenly an awareness of her nakedness in the face of death became an embarrassment, as in a dream in which she found herself unclothed at a ceremony, a funeral or a marriage, and she crossed her arms to hide her ash stained breasts. She watched as Ram lifted the body, held him in his arms like a groom heading for a threshold, and carried him out through the open door, into the night. Lisa heard nothing, but when Ram returned, his arms were empty.

She had never seen anyone killed before, not even the one she had herself dispatched with that heavy marble lion by accident in aiming for her husband. A quick glimpse at her face only. This time had been very different. He was insane of course, but this made little difference given her sense of wrong. What did make a difference was the expression on his face while Ram strangled him. He was smiling, enjoying it, wanting, she thought, to die.

She had tried to look away, sitting there naked on that chair, but she couldn't. She didn't hate him, but given what she'd been through and the quietly spoken promise of more, she thought it was right that the world be rid of him. Four and more women, he had told her, and that she would be the next. The distinct muscles in Ram's arms were pumping, his face, invisible to her, was pressed close to the man's, as if his indistinct words were seductive, as if he were about to kiss him. It had seemed he was looking at her, and maybe he was, almost ecstatic as blood leaked from his eyes, as if this were an orgasm and not the awareness of impending death.

She had fought him, but he had overpowered her and thrust a fist of cotton into her face. Ether. She had smelled it before, and when she awoke she was naked and had been tied to the chair. He stood in front of her, but not close, and he showed her his instruments, a surgical knife, a pair of pliers. He held them out on his palms, smiling and tilting his head to the side as if to say there is only this. Then he spoke to her, telling her that on this first day there would be only looking, that he would sit there—he'd gestured to the chair behind him—and look at her. All day and all night, he'd said, he'd be looking at her face, her hair, her breasts, her lovely naked shoulders. He would not touch her, not with his hands and these instruments. That would come later, that intimacy. "And, oh yes," he'd said. "There *are* a few other things." He'd reached in his pockets and taken out some small rubbery figures, doll's hands and feet, bald little heads. "There will be places for these as well," still smiling, looking at her, his eyes like little cups of gold, slightly unfocused. He'd taken the dark glasses off. "The better to see you."

And he'd sat there in his chair, fiddling with those doll parts throughout the day and into the night. When the sun was completely gone and it was dark, he'd risen briefly and lit the oil lamp, then placed it on a rickety table beside her. The light had awakened her from dozing. Still, he watched her, her face and body now illuminated. She couldn't see his eyes clearly, but she knew by his dim intense posture that he was still watching her. On and on. She was hungry and she wanted a smoke, but these common desires seemed to have no place in the circumstance. She became more curious than fearful. Then the coyly withheld promises for their dark future together would shock her away from her mind's drifting. Anger then, as well as terror. Ram, she thought, where are you?

Then came the knock on the door. The man's head jerked to the side, and he rose quickly and stuffed the dirty rag into her mouth and strapped it in place, then grabbed his cane and the oil lamp and went to the far wall and sat down there, waiting. Another knock, louder. Then the door was struck, the walls of the hut shaking. There was a brief pause before the door was struck again, then again, and finally there was a crack of wood at the frame and the door flew open, and there was Ram, standing in shadow beyond the sill. He started to enter, but the door had hit the wall, bounced off it, and hit Ram full in the face. He fell to the floor of the hut, then slowly rose up. There was blood on his face and he was shaking.

She sat on the bed in her room at the Sea Burst, going over it all once again, the killing and the aftermath. When Ram had unbound her, he hadn't looked at her naked body, robbing her of her modesty, and she had loved him for it. Then, after the monster was taken out into the night and she had lit another Djarum after dressing herself, she sat in her chair smoking and watched as Ram studied the places he might have touched and used one of the numerous rags cast about to wipe them clean. He had lifted the cane from the floor, wiped it too, and then had taken it out and disposed of it as he had the man. When he returned, he seemed satisfied, and he went to her and helped her up out of the chair and took her in his arms. He held her close for a few moments, then said it was time to go, and on the way out, the rag still in his hand, he pushed the door back into place as best he could, then slipped the lock through the hasp and secured it.

She remembered only vague images of their way down into the town. She'd stepped on something as she walked behind him on the narrow path, his hand reaching behind him to hold hers, something rubbery. It was late, and the town was almost empty, though she could hear sounds of activity in the amusement park and on the beach beyond, music and laughter. They passed a few revelers on their trip down main street. Then they arrived at the Sea Burst and he'd taken her up to her room. They'd sat on the bed together. He held her and kissed her and rubbed his hand against her back. Then they lay down facing each other and in awhile fell asleep.

They awoke in the middle of the night and agreed that they would have breakfast together come late morning. Then he left her. She missed him immediately. She hoped she could sleep what was left of the night away, and then it would be morning and she would see him once again.

CHAPTER 15

FRIDAY

Thursday night brought storm and wind. It had started up in Canada, then worked its way quickly down the coast, arriving at the town around two am. Most revelers were fast asleep. Fires on the beach had been dampened, yet a few coals sizzled still as the rain flooded down. The bars closed, and late drinkers, dressed in their skeleton costumes and soaked, made their way quickly down main street, heading for shelter at hotels and tents at the campground. Night lights flickered at the Sea Burst, but electrical power struggled, staying connected, and the night desk clerk found no reason to awaken her boss.

On the beach, a large rhinoceros broke free of its mooring. Packed with candy, it rose slowly, lifted by its helium balloons, then headed out over the churning waves, ten or more feet above them. A single boat holding thoroughly drunk celebrants rocked in its wake, and arms and sticks reached up to crack open the animal, but futilely, and the wild African figure continued, growing smaller, until it disappeared completely in darkness, approaching the sodden horizon. And down the beach, beyond the curve where the town disappeared, the dead man lay on his back, his body soaked. Sand had drifted to cover his arm and leg on his windward side, and his vacant eyes, awash, stared up into the low black clouds that passed quickly over him. Then the clouds took on a rosy glow and began to thin out and disperse. The wind quieted down, and by shortly after 5:00 am the sun began its ascent and the storm passed.

When Angelo awoke Friday morning, he felt vibrant and alive, as if that old-time weight had been lifted from his shoulders. His debt was paid, thanks to Ram, his hotel was ship-shape, he felt stronger in the muscles in his arms and legs than he had for almost two years. Maybe I should call for some drugs, he thought. Something mellow, and a little sex. Then he thought again. No, I don't need that right now.

He dressed in his best summer clothes, tan, loose linen pants, and a light brown cotton shirt, untucked at the waist. He'd combed his hair and applied a little scent, then, before he called down for his breakfast, he decided to see what might be happening down-stairs. Esperanza was ready at her counter.

"How are things going?" Angie said. "Any problems?"

"All in good order, Mr. Camp. No problems." Espe-ranza answered.

"Well thanks, Espe. I count on you, you know."

"No problem," Espe answered.

Next he went to the kitchen, clean and tidy, then the bar, where the piano lid was down, all the bot-tles carefully aligned on the shelves. The piano tuner would be coming around noon. From there he went to glance into his office, no mail, then made his way to the restaurant.

It was only seven, and the place held only a few diners, mostly couples and some singles, all sitting, as if by chance, at a good distance from one another. He looked around. Then his eyes hit upon a blonde woman, her hair cut short, somewhat severe, but even at this distance he could tell it was being left to grow out. A change is coming, he thought.

She wore a stretchy, short sleeve jersey that hugged her small breasts; she sat erect, her shoulders well back; one wrist, a thin gold bracelet, on the edge of the table. Time to eat, he thought, He crossed the room and moved to her table.

"I know you," he said with a smile.

"Well, you ought to," she said. "I'm staying in your hotel."

"No, no. Well, of course," he said, "But I was trying to remember another time."

"On the beach?"

"May have been. But really, it's no matter. I see you haven't eaten yet. Would you mind a companion?"

She agreed, and he sat down across from her, and the waitress came and they ordered, talking all the time. Where are you from? Have you been here long? Will you be staying on? Then, over the meal, and even after the plates were cleared away, they spoke of things that had to do with feelings, both surprised by their candor.

"Then my husband died, and I was alone and angry. My son was gone. I had a daughter that I had farmed out. I was enraged, and only in this week, just days ago, did I confront this amazing anger and begin to put it to rest."

"I had wanted to be a doctor, this young fool I was, studying restaurant management. I never did really try. It was the States. I was partying. Good at my job, it was not challenging, and I had plenty of time to waste my time. I have a good friend who is a doctor. I admire him."

And so it went. He watched her mouth move, a little oddly, when she spoke. He watched her blue eyes and looked into them. He was tall and thin, she thought, nice nose, that smile. His hands. Lovely long fingers, recently manicured and expressive.

He tried to think of her with drugs and sex. The sex was there, but the drugs made no sense at all. Here she was, in the clear light of morning. That was enough. He was hungry for her company.

He asked her if she would accompany him to dinner, not here, but someplace else, someplace quiet and romantic, and she agreed.

"And I won't bring my son or daughter!" She laughed, and he joined her in laughter.

Bright sunlight greeted Charly when he awakened at 6:30 am, already excited. He had slept soundly, warmed by his father's body through the night. They shared a bed at the Sea Burst, and he was careful to slip out from beneath the covers, so as not to wake him. Then he crept over to the closet and packed up his gear. He would meet Mrs. Hobby on the beach at noon. She would bring a lunch, and he would show her his wares: his magic tricks, his locks and magnets, and his fingerprint kit. He dressed, then sat in a chair and watched his father's body rise and fall under the covers. Wake up, he thought. Breakfast.

They ate in the hotel dining room, the place slowly filling up at 7:45 am. They both rushed a little. His father wanted to get to the clinic early, make sure things were in order, before he left to purchase some supplies in a nearby town, bandages, splints, and antiseptics.

"You can come with me, if you want, Charly," his father said.

"Okay," Charly said. "But I have to be back, to change and get to the beach before noon."

"Plenty of time," Ernesto answered.

And there was. And while his father unloaded the supplies and spent some time with Ram, who seemed a little unsettled this morning, Charly went back to the Sea Burst, put on his swimsuit and checked his gear, then headed to the amusement park and the beach to meet Edna Hobby.

Ram had never killed a man before. He was a doctor, and while a few patients had died under his caring hands and he had seen death and was familiar with it, to actively cause it, that was something else entirely. He'd spoken to the man, tried to make him understand, about his wife, his grief, about why he had to do this. But the man, this Hephaestus, hadn't seemed to understand. He'd just smiled, struggled a little, as Ram pressed his thumbs into his windpipe. It was that, as much as anything, this lack of understanding, that had driven him, his hands tight around the man's neck, squeezing until his forearms ached. Then it was over, and though he did have regrets, they were vague ones. His wife. He had avenged her, and he had to admit the certain freedom that he now felt. Finally, how odd, she was at rest, and he had begun to feel his grief and anger slowly lifting.

He arrived at the Sea Burst early, but she was already waiting for him, there at a table off to the side of the restaurant. He sat down, then reached across the table and took her hand. She was flushed, with both embarrassment and wonder, and his smile didn't sooth her.

"What should we do?" she asked, her voice a little shaky.

"Nothing," he said. Then he thought better of that curt answer.

"I mean, I don't know. It was bad. But it feels right."

"Yes," she said. "I agree." She choked back a laugh. "But will we ever get past it?"

"*I* will," he said. "You will too, I think, in time."

"And in the meantime?" she asked, her voice tentative.

"I love you," he said.

This time she did laugh, leaning back in her chair.

"But we just met!" she said. "I can't. But do you really?"

"Yes, really," he answered.

"Me too," she whispered.

They ordered their breakfast, bacon and eggs, whole wheat toast, coffee. They ate ravenously, glancing at each other shyly. He asked her about dinner, and she agreed. He asked her about staying on, and she demurred. Momentarily, he was hurt, but she smiled at him, and the hurt went away. To Florida?She said yes, but she could come back for a week or more before summer's end. She asked him if he would want that, and he grinned and shook his head vigorously in the affirmative. They were both careful of the other diners, not wanting to call any attention to themselves. But surely they see it, he thought, something between us. She thought the same, and flushed a little. When they had finished their meal and rose from their chairs, he took her in his arms, in sight of all the others, and kissed her. She didn't pull away.

The beach had changed its demeanor. A broad sandbar had risen up out of the swells only a few yards from shore, and children had waded out to it and were playing with plastic implements and shells. Schools of small fish darted around in the warm, narrow tributary between the beach and bar. All the piñatas had been damaged and now lay on the sand, balloons deflated, their bellies erupting with candy bones and small skeletal heads, and behind them the amusement park, though active with families at midday, had closed down certain rides for storm damage repair. Things, for some reason, were quieter than they had been in the previous days, revelers more subdued, swimmers and drinkers lackadaisical in their various endeavors, lying back as the surf washed over them, sipping only occasionally from bottles.

Edna was enjoying the magic, cards, scarves, and disappearing coins, and Charly was grinning at her interest. They had eaten their lunch, and were now talking between tricks, Charly sitting cross legged on the blanket, Edna in her low beach chair.

"And what about school? Charly. We haven't talked about that. And your sister and father."

"Well, first off, I like school a lot. I like to study, not just, I guess, my hobbies. Oops," he said. "That's your name!"

"Yes, it is," she said. "What a coincidence!" And they both laughed.

"I like science most of all. And I even like English, sometimes. And art and music."

"Isn't that about everything?"

"Yeah, I guess it is."

"Your father?"

"He's sad, you know. About my mother's death. He can't seem to get over it."

"That's hard, I'm sure."

"It is. But it's been a long time."

"It was a long time for me too. My husband."

He was silent for a moment, shuffling his deck of cards. He thought he should say something, but he didn't know what. Edna saw this and changed the subject.

"How about your sister? Rosa, right?"

"Yes, Rosa. She's not my friend, or anything like that, and she likes to get into my stuff. Otherwise, she's okay. She's away at camp right now. Her first time. We talked on the phone. She's having fun."

And the talk went on. And then, around two o'clock, Edna suggested they talk a walk down the beach, maybe find some shells or something.

"Have you been there?" she asked.

"Not yet," Charly answered.

"Neither have I," said Edna. And so they started out, walking into a soft, gentle breeze, leaving the Day of the Dead behind.

The stormy sea had thrown up various items onto the sand at shore line. A broken lobster trap, various piece of driftwood and lumber, a dead gull, and both Edna and Charly stopped to examine them, poking with a long twisted stick Charly had salvaged on their way. There were shells too, and though they lifted and examined them, there was nothing they thought interesting enough to keep. A small coil of wire Charly offered to Edna. She declined and he tucked it into the shoulder bag that held his gear.

"Look at this," Edna said, offering him a miniature tool of some kind. It looked like a small nut pick.

"And this," Charly said. It was a rain ruined snapshot depicting a young blonde girl, her face half washed away.

They proceeded slowly along the beach and in a while rounded the broad curve. Then Charly heard something in the distance, a hum of sound, and Edna Hobby heard it too.

"What *is* that?" she said.

"Animal," Charly answered.

They stopped, lifted their hands to their brows to block out the bright sun, and gazed down the beach. Something. A kind of roiling, as if the sand had come alive and was vibrating. Then the sound they had first heard became clearer as it approach. A bleating.

"Sheep!" Charly said, as they stood there and watched the mob approaching. They covered the entire beach, narrower now after the storm, and they saw the figure of a man walking on the high side, a tall staff in his hand, gently urging the animals forward.

Then the sheep reached them where they stood their ground and began to flow around them, at times brushing their bare legs with their wooly coats. They smelled pungent but good, and both turned to each other and smiled. At the end of the mob walked the shepherd. A Mexican, Edna thought, or could he be, how to explain it here? A Basque? The man was not smiling, but he didn't look unfriendly.

"Good morning," Edna said.

"*No hablo Ingles. Solo un poco,*"the man said. "*Pero...*" He held up his hand, indicating they should not proceed.

"Hell! Of course you damned well do!" Edna answered, then caught herself as Charly looked over at her inquisitively.

"I mean, come on. It's okay. What's the problem? Where are you going?"

"*Adonde vas?*" Charly asked, conversationally.

" *Me voy a la montana,*" the man answered.

"*Pero por que?*" Charly said, and Edna, her mouth open in wonder, listened to this conversation she did not understand.

The man spoke for a while, and Charly asked questions and made comments. At one point he laughed, but after a while his face darkened, his questions becoming more urgent and serious. Then, in a while, their conversation seemed to be winding down. The man had been waving his arms and gesturing. Then he seemed to give it up, whatever it was.

"*Me tengo que ir,*" he said.

"*Bueno,*" Charly answered.

The shepherd moved off through the mob then, and when he reached the front, he poked his staff into the rump of the leader and he and his sheep moved slowly along the beach, heading for the town.

"What did he say?" Edna asked, still a little stunned at Charly's evident skill with the language. This is some kid, she thought.

"A lot," Charly said. "He said he was hired to cut down the ski trails. The sheep are like lawn cutters. Those are his words, and they made me laugh. But more importantly, he said there is a dead man down the beach, a little way. Then he said he must be going."

"A dead man?" Edna said.

"Yes," Charly answered. "That's exactly what he said. Dead as a door knob. He meant a nail. Will we go on?" He looked up at Edna.

She smiled. "Of course we'll go on," she said, though she was a little uncertain about taking Charly on such an expedition. Well, why not? She thought. We've come this far. We're together in this. Still, is this the right thing? He's so young.

Charly caught her concern. "I've seen death," he said. "Animals. And twice, when my father took me through the hospital, the human ones, an old man, and a woman killed in an accident. It's okay. Come on, let's go."

And so they did. They moved along the beach to where the cliff rose up high above them and in a short while came upon the body. It was tucked down into the sand, and all around it, from the bank well down to the edge of the receding surf, where shallow hoof holes that the sheep had left behind. The man's eyes were wide open and lightly glazed over. In the bright sun, they looked like tiny cups of melted gold. A smile touched his lips, bizarre in this circumstance, and both stared down into those eyes, realizing nothing at all was there. The body seemed to rest peacefully. It was not twisted, and though they saw bruises on his arms and cheeks, he didn't seem otherwise damaged. And yet, both saw the band of redness on his throat.

"Strangled," Charly said. "And I know him."

"What!?" Edna said.

"Well I don't actually *know* him. But I met him on the beach. He was very strange."

"We have to report this," Edna said.

"Sure we do. Should we go now?"

"Not just yet," she answered. "Charly, do you have your magnets?"

"Yes. Here in my bag. But isn't this what they call a crime scene? Should we mess with it?"

"The sheep have destroyed any evidence, I think. And we won't touch the body. Let's just see what the sand close by has to offer."

Charly then removed his largest neodymium magnet from the bag, and placing it here and there in the sand surrounding the body, began to pull things into its orbit: not much, a bobby pin, what looked like a crushed and rusted belt buckle, a nail from a ruined lobster trap. Edna stood above him, watching, as he opened his search wider. He was near the edge of the rise, when both saw something large moving toward them under a half inch of sand, the sand rippling like an ocean swell. When it got to them, Charly lifted the magnet, and there, attached to it at a heavy metal band, was a cane.

"Don't touch it," Edna said.

"Okay," Charly said. "I'll just free it." And using the buckle he pushed it away from the magnet, and it fell lightly in the sand. Then he glanced up at Edna. "Fingerprints?" he said.

"Out here?" she said. "After last night's storm?"

"Well, sometimes," Charly answered. "You'd be surprised."

He opened up his bag then and removed his finger print kit, and lifting a small plastic bottle, sprinkled a powdery substance along the cane's length. Then he produced a magnifying glass, got back down on his knees, blew the substance away, and began his study.

"You're Sherlock Holmes," Edna laughed, then fell silent, realizing the inappropriateness of her joke.

"Not really," Charly said, more serious than she.

"So, what are you finding, Charly?"

"Nothing," he said. "There are no prints. But I think it's been wiped clean. And look at this." He gestured for Edna to join him, and she lowered herself to her knees and looked where he pointed. There was an inscription cut into the broad metal band a few inches below the handle, just the one word, Aphrodite.

"Goddess of Love," Edna said softly.

"I know that," Charly said, to Edna's surprise. "I've read about her."

"But look there, at his wrist," Edna said. "What is that?"

"A charm bracelet," Charly said. "Those little gold things? Girls in school wear them."

They stood up, leaving the cane where it was, looked down once again at the body, and Charly started to leave, but Edna touched him on the shoulder.

"Look up there," she said, pointing above them to the cliff's edge, where the small hut was lit brightly by the sun.

"Do you think he came from there?" Charly asked.

"Well, his body was soaked, but that was most probably the rain. And he was too far up on the beach to have come out of the sea. And, anyway, we're sure he was strangled, aren't we? And the cane. It was well back near the cliff's face. I think we have to go up there, Charly, after we report this."

"But the police," Charly asked. "Should we tell them?"

"Oh, they'll figure it out soon enough. But I'd like to get there first. What do you say?"

"*Vamonos,*" Charly answered.

When they returned to the town, they told no one, but went directly to the police station and reported the death to the desk officer.

"Are you sure?" he asked.

"Sure as hell," Edna replied.

"Okay," he said. "We'll want to question you two. Where are you staying?"

They told him, and he continued.

"Nobody must know," he said. "Not your parents, young man, nor any relatives, Mrs. This could cause a mess in town, what with all these shenanigans. And we can't have that. Mums the word. Go home, I mean to your hotel. We'll be in touch."

But they didn't return to the Sea Burst, not immediately, but headed for the dune path that led up to the hut at the cliff's edge. It took them no more than a half hour to get there, and when they looked down over the cliff they saw policemen clomping around on the beach, one sticking poles into the sand and stringing yellow tape around the body, quite a few feet from it. They watched as an ambulance approached, its tires flattened in order to negotiate the sand. Then they turned away from the cliff's edge and moved to the door, which was secured by a big lock.

"Wanna go to work?" Edna asked, and Charly in answer removed the picks from his bag, knelt down at the door, and began to fiddle with the lock. In moments he had it, and after they'd pushed at the door, which was wedged in tight at the frame, and opened it, they stood on the brink of the strange room. They did not enter.

"What a mess," Charly said. "And all those pictures on the wall. And those ropes and tape."

"These are dark things," Edna said. "Best not consider them too much."

But they didn't leave immediately. They stood there and looked around the room. A surgical knife and a pair of pliers sat on a table. Pieces of duct tape hung from a chair, and another chair had fallen on its side. Only the pictures on the wall seemed untouched. A young woman, both as a child and as an adult, and numerous other, very dark, things.

"Do you think that might be Aphrodite?" Charly asked, recalling the name cut into the cane's metal ring.

"I don't know," Edna answered. She was looking at the floor near the edge of the chair holding the strips of tape. A cigarette butt. Djarums, she said to herself. Lisa has been here.

CHAPTER 16

APHRODITE, 8:00 pm

Now that my father is taken care of, no longer any rage or sadness for his ghost to count on, there are only a few things left to consider. This walking for example. Then to spend some of the money left to me that I've been hoarding. Maybe a winter trip to the Islands? I can't be sure, but something. I've been too long in this place without respite. Then the name change, getting rid of this past as far as I'm able. My mother was Ann. That will be the first one, and I've decided on something simple and direct for the last. That's Brown. Ann Brown. Somebody else entirely. Exactly who I think I'll be.

Then there is the question of how to deal with Ram Chopra, Lisa, Edna and Charly. That will all work out: the growing love between Ram and Lisa, Edna's involvement with Angelo, and the sweet innocence of Charly.

But this walking. I'm tired now as I approach the back streets of the town, no longer feeling perused, nothing behind me to urge me on. And I think now, without trepidation, that I might ride back on the bus, sitting still in a window seat, watching vague images passing in the night, at times my face reflected in the glass with the question of who I'll be then. Has it come to nothing, these years of walking? I won't say that, since I've had a life in spite of it. I've memorized my often trod ways, taken in a world that was given, in spite of my not having selected it. Maybe we all are walking, from place to place, comings and goings, always working to get there. But how many of us are aware? Do we mark the passage with sight, or hear the changing sounds surrounding us as we make our way? Or is this all philosophical nonsense, these ruminations. Maybe. I'm not sure. In that way I haven't been sure of most anything in my journey.

Patricide. A sick, maddening thing on the face of it. But then the particulars. Ram Chopra free of his rage, and, with Lisa, maybe free of his ongoing, obsessive mourning as well. And I? I'm free of that dull and continuous anxiety, always there, under every gesture and the passage of those few words spoken to others, maybe even of this walking. My feet are tough, but I am not. I'm worn out, slowing down, all to the good. I might have loved him, but it was love born of cruelty and torture. Those butchered women, all surrogates for me, and in a way I carried the guilt for their suffering in me. I had seen that in his eyes even before he killed them. It was that twisted, penetrating look holding their future in dark glee that ruined me, even as I was but a child, always, and loved in weird ways impossible to understand, even now. But enough of these ruminations. So onward.

A few bedraggled revelers have spilled out of the ongoing celebrations as I trudge on. Members of a mariachi band, two trumpets and an accordion, play softly against their nature on a stoop below a porch light, which is lit now that night is coming on. A skeleton family passes by me, somewhat resolutely, heading back to some lodging I have passed and is now behind me. Horns, laughter, and singing echo faintly from a distance, and I am approaching the place of thatturning that will take me up to Main Street and all the remaining activity. The bars may be packed, but on the streets the day's celebrations will be coming to a gradual ending. Children must get to bed. Parents must leave with them. Only childless adults will remain. All this is okay with me. I'll be able to keep up my pace without too much physical interference. I'll probably make a loop, walking out beyond the campground near the ski-trail mountain, then heading back beside the beach until I turn into town and walk to the bus station. I've no idea of the schedules, but that's okay. I can try to sit and wait for the next one, see if I can manage that. I believe I can now. We'll see.

I have no wish for anything but the following: I would like to lay naked and relaxed on the beach under the sun; I would like to wake in the morning at peace, with no urge for walking; I would like to eat dinner at a fine restaurant, at an outdoor table under an awning in a foreign city, perhaps Paris, a decent man sitting across from me, smiling. And these things can happen. I'll just have to wait a while for them.

Main Street. Pink cotton candy still spinning onto plastic wands, a man with a beard, in a skeleton suit, laughing as he tries to eat it. Hangers holding costumes being lifted from metal racks and taken into closed down shops. A marzipan bone dealer pushing his cart slowly among a crowd of revelers who seem to be fighting their exhaustion. The end is coming, and I'm sure most of the town fathers, the doctor, the police, will be glad for it, their town once again as peaceful as it ever gets in summer.

I am coming to the end of Main, where the street becomes a rugged road twisting off toward the campground and the mountain. It's darker here, no lights to guide me, but I don't need any, having been here many times before. A single drunk lies in brush at roadside, quietly snoring. Otherwise there are only a few bird songs, the gentle sound of surf in the distance, my breathing. Then, just as I think it's almost over, there's this woman Natasha, intended as only a bit player. What in the world is she doing here? Things are getting out of hand.

Chapter 17

STILL FRIDAY

The police arrived at the Sea Burst at 5:00 pm. Edna, Charly and his father were waiting in Angie's office to the side of the lobby. Comfortable chairs, and Angie had placed a pitcher of iced tea, glasses and lemons, on a tray upon his desk. The police chief had come himself, together with two other policemen, ones who had been at the crime scene earlier in the day.

Edna had spoken to Angie upon their return and had told him of their discovery.He had right away seen to a late lunch, sandwiches and fruit, and had then escorted the two up to Edna's room.

"Should I phone your father?" he said to Charly, and Edna had answered.

"That's okay. I'll see to that."

"Well, okay," Angie said, then hesitantly, "Should we call off our dinner?"

"Not at all!" Edna responded, smiling. "Meet you downstairs at seven?"

"Fine," Angie said. "That's just fine." Then he left.

Edna sat on the edge of her bed, Charly in a chair by the window.

"The police will be coming," she said. "What should we say? Should we tell them everything?"

"I don't know," Charly said. "What do you think?"

"Well, we shouldn't lie, you know. The police after all. But maybe we might leave things out. Maybe the cane. Maybe our trip to the hut. Does that make sense to you?"

"That wouldn't be lying, then," he said. "Just leaving things out."

"Oh, but Charly," she said. "Really it would be lying. At least the way they'd see it. I'm the adult here. I should make the decision and not put it on you."

"But I see it clearly," he said. "And I don't think it would be doing wrong. It didn't really interfere with anything."

"No. It didn't," she said. But for that cigarette, she thought. But Charly didn't know about that. She'd picked it up. It would be her lie, not his.

"Okay," she said. "The cane and the hut. The rest is as we discovered it."

"All the news that's fit to print," Charly answered. "That's from the *New York Times*!"

It almost amounted to nothing. The chief asked them about the shepherd, and they told him what they knew, which was very little, and one of the other officers wrote down the gist of their answers. Then the chief brought up the subject of the crime scene, had they approached the body, had they touched anything.

"With our hands?" Charly asked.

"Well, of course!" the chief said. "How else would you touch something?"

"Okay," Edna said, glancing at Charly, "No, we didn't touch anything."

"There's the question of the cane," one of the officers chimed in.

"I *know* that," the chief bristled. "I was getting to that."

The officer shrugged and looked away.

"How is it, do you think, that the cane sat on the sand after the storm. A person was half buried, after all."

"Not quite," Edna said. "Just a drift against his arm and leg."

"Yes, yes," the chief responded. "But there was no such drift against the cane."

"A cane is lighter than a man," Charly said. "The wind could have pushed it. Above the sand, I mean."

"That could be," the officer chimed in again, and the chief looked long and hard at him.

"We didn't touch it," Edna said, looking long and hard at the chief, and Charly nodded vigorously.

"Okay," the chief said, "That will be enough." He looked over at the two officers. "Have either of you got any questions?" He was staring them down, and neither one had anything more to say.

And so the meeting ended, and after Edna had shaken Charly's hand and that of his father, she smiled at Charly, said "See you soon, young man!" and headed to her room to get ready for dinner with Angie.

Ernesto put his hand on Charly's shoulder at they left the Sea Burst. He had a few things left to do at the clinic, and he didn't want to leave Charly alone.

"You did good, Charly," he said as they made their way down main street, slipping between those still cavorting. "Are you okay? I mean about the dead body and all."

"Yes," Charly said. "Just a little tired is all."

Ernesto finished up at the clinic, and when they got back to the hotel it was just after seven. Charly lay down on the bed and was soon asleep. Ernesto sat in a chair facing the bed, watching his son breathe.

I should call Rosa, he thought, and even with her name in his mind, almost on his lips, thoughts of that other Rosa came upon him, words of remembered conversations, their walking together on that path frequented by Charly and his sister on their way back from school. Let me put you away, he thought, into the peace of your death. He had no belief in an afterlife, but he did believe the dead remained alive in memory, so long as the memories were not longing, but rather a kind of celebration of times spent together. He still missed her. It was true. But sitting there, watching his beautiful son sleeping, thinking of his vibrantly cheerful daughter, he felt that there might be a future in view for all of them. He felt he might be able to leave his dear wife behind, as they had, in her presence in all his waking hours, though never in memory. It's a little late, he thought, she'll be busy with games and things, and soon she'll be sleeping, just as Charly is. I'll try her tomorrow.

Then he picked up a book he'd been reading for close to a month. It was a fat Russian novel, and given that he had put it aside for more than two weeks, he was lost when it came to the difficult names and which characters they belonged to. Still, he worked his way back slowly into the story.

And what of Edna Hobby? She had showered and shaved her legs and was then sitting in front of the mirror, applying her makeup. Very subtle, she thought, not too much. She felt an itch in her inner thigh. Already we have become fast friends, well not quite that, she thought. Could a plan be in the works? Foolish woman. It's just dinner, some dark and intimate place, he'd said. Oh, my. Oh, my! Am I getting myself into something?

Something else. She and Charly had pulled it off, so to speak, but she still felt a little uneasy. He was just a little boy, after all. Have I used him? But there was no gain, just inquisitiveness, his as well as hers, and in fact he'd seemed delighted in the adventure, bringing his skills into play. Oh, let it alone, she thought. If I need to come clean, for both of us, I'll do so when the time comes. He really has brought joy back into my life.

But now there was another reason to be uneasy. After the police interview, she'd gone to Lisa's room, and without any small talk, had confronted her with the discovery of her cigarette butt, a telltale Djarum, in that strange hut.

Lisa broke down briefly, then gathered herself, and told her mother the whole story.

"He kept me bound up in there, for a long time," she said. "I was naked, and he told me what he was going to do to me. He was just looking at me then, fiddling with those instruments, the whole day and into the night.It was horrible. Then Ram came. That evil bastard had killed his wife, as well as other women. He'd tortured them! Ram. I love him, mother! I really do."

She fell, weeping hysterically, into her mother's arms then, and Edna held her and soothed her, something they both recognized as a rare event.

"There, there, my daughter. I am with you," Edna said. She felt a sob of release deep in her stomach. It didn't quite make it to her throat.

CHAPTER 18

SUNDAY

ON FRIDAY THE SHEEP HAD ARRIVED, CAUSING HYSTERIA but little havoc on the beach. The shepherd had smiled, calm in his slow driving of the mob in their movement toward the ski trails on the mountain. Their hooves pockmarked the beach, but it was only those who attempted to move away, for some reason frightened, that momentarily slowed the march. Their bones danced on their bodies, but the sheep took no interest in these animated skeletons. The shepherd whistled and spoke softly to the leader, until things were back in order. Those who just stood or sat there, enjoyed the dark, musky smells as the mob flowed in its wooly river around them. Once they were gone, in the wake of the spirit dampening storm of Thursday night and the discovery of the body, energy came back strongly, as well as energizing curiosity. People speculated about the death in gatherings on the beach and in the amusement park. Local shopkeepers moved from store to store for gossip. And there was dancing and music on the beach in the day, and it got more serious and jubilant by nightfall—beach fires, games played by children in the warm surf. The piñata balloons were re-inflated, and those large animals rose up once again into the starry sky.

Then, on Saturday morning, the storm returned again. The sky darkened, and rain pounded the town. There were brief, teasing interludes of clearing and sun, then the dark clouds rolled in again and the rain continued its onslaught. Spirits dipped as did the piñatas, once again deflated and on their sides on the beach, their swollen bellies an invitation that, in the rain, was not accepted. Vendors packed up their gear. Those in the campground put away their sodden tents and started their RV's. And a good portion of the Day of the Dead celebrants checked out of their motels and hotels, and headed for home. Angelo's hotel was no exception. Most of his guests check out, some arguing for a refund of Sunday's room fee. Angie accommodated them. They'd had a taste of the town and its offerings, and he expected that a portion would return to his hotel in the future.

Half the rides and games in the amusement park were covered with tarps, and only a few solitary figures rode and played at those that remained in service. Main Street was dark in the storm, and though most of the stores remained open, there were few customers in them.

The drunks were out in force, untouched, in their delirium, by neither rain nor wind. Though many stayed in the bars, others staggered down the streets or sat on benches, looking up into the rain that pelted their soaked, flushed faces. The Day of the Dead was not over, and yet it seemed to be. Late Saturday night, the storm slowly moved out to sea, though not many were witness to its leaving. Then came Sunday, bright sun and warm air, though only a few were left to enjoy it.

Bo and Ned lay on the beach. It was quiet now, only the pleasing sound of a few adults and the light laughter of children playing in the water, the beach close to empty. They had applied lotion to each other, and Ned had brought a small umbrella from the Sea Burst in order to guard their faces from the warm sun, and Bo had packed a lunch and a good bottle of Pinot Gris. They were not eating as of yet as it was only 9:00 am. They lay on their backs, looking up into the umbrella's spokes, talking.

"The Day of the Dead seems dead," Bo said.

"Will you be leaving?" Ned asked. He didn't want to bring that up.

"Well, no, actually," Bo answered. "I've spoken to Camp at the hotel. He's fully booked now that summer is getting underway, and he could use a piano player. The money's okay, though those skeleton people have been poor tippers. It's nice here, and I have nowhere else I need to be. What about you?"

"Well, I could stay," Ned answered. "I'd like to do more drawing, then get some paints and canvases and start painting. I've been thinking about a series, both drawing and paintings, self-portraits, and portraits of you too. What do you think?"

Bo was touched in a way that was unimaginable before coming to the town and to Ned. His arrogance and cold hearted nature had begun to dissolve. He didn't miss it. He was happy for the first time in a long while.

"I think it's a great idea. And I think it would be very good to spend more time together."

"So do I," Ned said. "I mean about the time."

They both laughed lightly.

Bo raised up on the blanket, thinking to give Ned a little kiss, but then he spied activity a short way down the beach.

"What is that?" he said, and Ned rose up too and turned to see what Bo was looking at.

A boxy canvas structure, a tent that looked more like a small room, four or five times the size of an outhouse and multi-colored, sat, lightly vibrated by the gentle breeze, ten or so yards back from the shore curls at the warm water's edge. A directors chair had been settled into the sand facing the sea, and a man sat in it, his back to them, fiddling with something in his lap. Another man stood to the side of the chair, a clipboard in his hand. At times he would bend over, giving his chubby body a posture suggesting vulnerability. And across on the other side of the canvas structure, so hidden that they could only guess at the happenings there, the head and shoulders of a woman appeared. She lifted something made of fabric, inserted a hanger, and slid the hanger onto something that was out of sight. And three men were raking the sand, removing leftover sheep evidence and human footprints. Soon the sand all around the trio of people and their fabric house had been smoothed out and now seemed almost like a tan carpet, the workers applying the back sides of their rakes in the task.

"A photo shoot," Ned said.

"Of course!" Bo said. "How could I have missed that?"

"She's inside. Or he is. Or they both are."

"It'll be a dramatic surprise," Bo said, and Ned laughed.

Then the canvas flap that was the door was thrown open, and a very tall, statuesque woman stepped out, barefoot, into the sand.

"My God, she's tall," Bo said.

And she was, six feet, two inches barefoot, and could get much taller, at least six four in heels. Dressed in a swimsuit with a semi-transparent garment draped around her, she stood there, waiting, her face in profile. It was an angular face, a thin, prominent nose, and lips that had been very well done: heavy, a slight pout, a good set of teeth when she smiled. She was very beautiful, this beauty only enhanced by the added character age provided. She was forty-three, and she looked like a goddess, delivered here from some unknown mythology.

She turned her head, seeing the photographer rise from his chair. They could then see her full face.

"Oh my God!" Ned sad, "It's Natasha!"

"Who?" Bo asked.

"You don't want to know," said Ned, remembering their last, brief conversation. What had she called him? Shitty face, among other things.

The photographer was ready, and the chubby clipboard assistant had removed his shoes and socks and rolled his pants legs to the knees, revealing white bony legs almost appropriate for the Day of the Dead. He stood in the quiet surf, took the model's hand and helped her to enter the water, though she needed no help at all. When she was up to her knees, she turned and shook out her long dark hair. Her gown was wet at the hem, and she looked carefree and in control at the same time. She placed her hands on her hips, tilted her head in mock impatience, and waited for the photographer to get started.

Both Bo and Ned watched her.

Natasha Burmakin was born into a farming family near the town of Lev Tolstoy, formerly Astapovo, renamed after Leo Tolstoy died there in 1910. Even as a child she was very tall, five-ten by the time she entered high school, where she took no interest in her studies, but for the English she was intent on learning, though to no avail. Already at fifteen, her plans were made. She would leave this place, school and the stink of farming, and would travel to America where she would become a famous fashion model with a new name, Natasha Burm. She was gangly, a bit awkward on her feet, and her fellow students, including her two sisters, made fun of her. Her brothers, however, left her alone. They were busy with their father on the farm. This would be their future, and they knew it.

"And so, Natasha, what is it this weather today?"

"I, it am cold, do I know."

Her fellow students would laugh at her then, ask another question in English, then laugh again.

By the time she began her senior year, having managed by the skin of her teeth to pass from grade to grade, she had gained control of her body. She no longer slumped at her shoulders, trying to shrink down enough to join others, but stood tall, and moved with considerable grace through the school's halls. Because of her height, she was invited to join the volleyball team. She was tempted. It would be good for her body, but she finally decided against it. Some my fingers, she thought in English, to have no broke of the hand.

So she graduated, last in her class and without honors, then packed her things and headed for the sea to a boat she'd found out about, a tanker that would provide cheap passage to America. She had enough money, though there was little in her family. Just enough to get by. The passage was rough, and she was tossed about in her small cabin where she spent most of the trip, avoiding the eyes of deckhands who clearly wished to spend valuable time with her.

When she arrived in New York City, she found lodging in a lower east side rooming house, and set out for the various talent agencies. Her English was abysmal, but that was not a problem. As long as she looked right and could take photographers' directions, she had a shot at becoming the tall, exotic flower in fine clothing and swimwear that the fashion industry was clamoring for. It took some time, but not that much, and after a short while she found herself with an agency contract and a few jobs that brought in a good deal of money. She moved to an apartment, furnished it with second-hand gear, and began her career in earnest. It took just a year for her to get a job wearing the clothing of a top designer at a winter mountain shoot in Aspen, coats and hats that were a reminder of the Russia she had left behind, and she wore them with such panache that the fashion industry was taken by storm. At least she thought of it that way. What really happened was that she was offered more jobs, not as a supermodel by any means, but a distinctive one nonetheless.

So the years went by, many jobs, a little bit of fame, plenty of money, two failed marriages. Those stupidy were fool bums. And yet her English improved until she could carry on limited conversations.

Then, early in her thirties, which was the way with models, the jobs came more infrequently, and the ones that did come dressed her in more matronly clothing, though she was still a little too young for that. She found herself neither here nor there, and for a while she was forced to live on her savings. Then, as she approached forty, she was reduced to hand, leg and foot jobs. This was when she met Ned and started up a relationship with him. She liked it that he was an artist. She didn't like it that he was often too busy with art and not attentive enough to her. Attention meant fine restaurants, clubs, and weekend vacations to what for her were exotic places. Finally, she told him to get lost, and it was the morning after their brief phone conversation that her agent called with a good job offer, swimsuits and beachwear for the mature woman at a small resort town up north. Reservations were provided, and she packed a large suitcase full of clothing for various occasions, then took a taxi to the airport.

They watched her as she cavorted in the surf, striking various poses, smiling and pouting. This went on for a half hour at least, then, all of a sudden, a buff, close to middle-aged man in a Speedo stepped out of the tent and went into the surf to stand beside her. He seemed a little younger than she, but no boy-toy, and once the photographer had given his directions, the two leaned close to each other, smiling suggestively. Then she threw her long arms into the air. He rested his hand on her bare hip. The photographer urged them on.

"A lot of work there," Bo said.

"Yeah," Ned said. "And a lot of money too."

"How much do you think?"

"Oh, I don't know. Maybe ten, twenty thousand. She would never say."

"That much, huh? How long were you together."

"About a year, I think. Oh, God!She's spied me."

She was striding up out of the surf where the assistant held up a large towel for her. She took it, wrapped herself in it, then, squinting a little in the sun, leaned forward. Then she lifted her palm to her brow like an Indian in one of those old cowboy movies. Her full mouth formed an O, and she grinned and wiggled her fingers and headed down the beach towards where they lay on towels in the sand. Ned tried to struggle to his feet, but she got there before he could rise. He was only up on his elbows when she arrived and looked down at him, her body blocking the sun. She reached down and tapped him under the chin with her long fingers.

"So this small boy shitty face, what is it Mr. Ned is here coming of course? Natasha must have to know." She looked over at Bo. "Who are you two doing in this place?"

"What," Ned said and immediately regretted having spoken.

"What?" Natasha said.

"Oh, nothing," Ned answered, looking away.

"Well, if nothing, why has this been spoke, this little word of no things? So, let us come on without it. Now answer." She jabbed her index finger into Ned's shoulder, hard, and a white circle appeared in his sun flushed skin, then slowly faded away.

"I'm here to do some drawing and painting."

"Painting?" she said. "What about plastic people of lines, those things built up into cages and stuff like this? And who is this handsome fellow here beside?"

"This is Bo," he said, raising his hand half heartedly and gesturing toward his now significant other. "We met in the city and found we were both coming here."

Natasha recognized his lie immediately. "So," she said. "These two of you are together. I am right?"

Ned started to speak, but she held up her hand to stop him.

"This was okay," she said. "I am liking homoerotica men. Many are into my business. That one I have touched in water? He is one. This fat little man also too. Not photographer. Soon he is call me. At end he is crazy at things he has wish to do whatever is wanted, by him."

"But we're just friends," Ned said, almost whining.

"Oh, come it on, Big Boy. Natasha, she knows! Where have you come to be staying here?"

"A place called the Sea Burst," Bo said, seeing that Ned was completely out of sorts.

"You say this!," Natasha laughed. "Me also too! I will see you there then. Tonight. We will drink it up!" Then the photographer called her over to begin the last shoot of the day.

He had gathered up a few skeleton figures and a few children also sporting bones, and he directed both Natasha and her partner to get into the surf with them. Then he told them to cavort as they wished. At first the children stood there in uncertainty and wonder, but once the adults took the directions and began to splash and dance, they too joined in. Natasha threw her arms around like a lunatic, and her partner did his best to keep up. The photographer clicked away, then motioned to his assistant to join the group. He did so with much enthusiasm, dancing, then falling down into the surf, soaking himself, then rising up again, water streaming from his head, in order to continue frolicking.

"Give it us your shooting!" Natasha screamed as she turned, her hair still dry and flying about her face, and Ned and Bo took the opportunity to pack up their stuff and steal away. They headed for town and a small, out-of-the-way-park, and there they sat down and ate their lunch in peace.

It was mid-morning when Edna Hobby tripped coming out of a shop on Main Street and fell onto the sidewalk injuring her right ankle. She was carrying a long garment bag containing a nice new dress, and the bag landed on top of her, covering her head and shoulders.

Though life on the street was now sparse, most of the Day of the Dead revelers having left in storm on the previous day, some of the shops had remained open, no longer stocked with celebratory costuming, but displaying the conventional clothing that comprised the bulk of their summer business.

Edna, struggling to free herself of the bag, called out loudly, but no one was there to hear her. Finally she managed to climb to her foot, the other lifted slightly and dangling in the air. There was blood on the arm she'd landed on and she felt more seeping out of her hair, licking her neck. Then, erect and angry at herself, she yelled out more forcefully.

"Son of a bitch! Someone come and help me!"

This desperate call was heard by the store owner, who skipped down the steps leading up to his door and helped Edna hop up and into his shop. He sat her down carefully in the "husband's chair" and went into the back and called the clinic.

"No need for an ambulance," he said. "But you'll need a car."

And that car was driven by Angelo Camp, who'd received a call from Ram Chopra, Lisa in the seat beside him.

"Mother, are you okay!"

"Yes, yes. But this foot will need some work."

Angelo lifted her into his arms and placed her in the front seat, and as he carried her, Lisa saw the smile on her mother's face over his shoulder. They drove to the clinic and were met at the door by Ram. He pushed a wheelchair down the ramp beside the steps, and the two men, one on each side, lifted Edna and placed her in it. She seemed to enjoy the attention.

There was some gentle manipulation, some bandaging of arm and head, and an x-ray, and when Ram came out of the darkroom in his heavy apron, he announced the verdict.

"No break," he said. "But a severe sprain. I'll soft cast it, and you'll have to ice it and keep it elevated."

"I better not travel," Edna said.

"Oh, no, that's okay. You can do that."

"I don't think so," Edna responded, smiling at Angie. Ram caught the look.

"Oh, well, maybe you're right. Best to keep it stationary."

They took the wheelchair with them, folded up in the trunk, and once they were back at the Sea Burst and Angie had settled Edna into it, a blanket, which she didn't really need, draped over her lap and legs, all three sat in Angie's office.

"I'll stay, mother," Lisa said.

"But you have jobs back in Florida," Edna said. "There's no need for that."

"That's right," Angie chimed in.

"I can cancel them," Lisa said. "I'll care for you."

"Absolutely not," Edna said, in her sharp abandoned voice, then caught herself and smiled. "Angie will look after me. Isn't that right, Angie?"

"Of course," he said. "For sure. No problem."

And so it was settled. Lisa would leave, on schedule, that afternoon. She had two weddings and a graduation party back in Tallahassee. The trip to the peninsula had cost her, and she needed to replenish her bank account.

"I'm going to go see Ram," she said, and she left the two of them, Angie fetching a cool lemonade for Edna and asking her what she'd like for lunch.

The two sat in Ram's apartment above the clinic. Lisa had told him that she was leaving, but that she could come back later in the summer for a week or so.

"How about a month," Ram said.

Lisa laughed. "Don't know if I can swing that. But maybe."

"That would be very good," he said.

They spent the next few minutes talking tentatively about a possible future, and before Lisa left, Ram took her in his arms and kissed her.

"I'll phone," she said, when he released her.

"So will I," Ram said.

Once Lisa had left—he'd walked her to the clinic door and held her hand on parting—Ram went back up to his apartment and gathered all the autopsy and crime scene materials, tucked them into a couple of fresh folders, together with the locket he'd worn around his neck since his wife's death, and shut them away in the small file cabinet he kept under his desk. It's finished now, he thought, even the killing of that monster is. Then he went online and began a search for possible positions in Tallahassee and the towns close by. I'm tired of this place, he told himself. Maybe I need a new view.

The Day of the Dead effectively ended before its conclusion. Most had left town in Saturday's storm or early Sunday morning, and though Sunday brought bright sun and a cloudless sky, the streets of the town were for the most part empty. The mayor, a Mexican-American accountant who had emigrated to this country from Chihuahua when he was a child, flags waving in a light breeze behind him, gave a brief speech to an audience that could be counted on toes and fingers. Slumped and bedraggled, their bones having slipped from articulation, they looked like surviving victims of a train wreck in some lost land. Though attentive, their applause after the Mayor's last words produced no more than the sounds made by the small hands of sleepy children following story time at the library.

By early afternoon, at the Sea Burst, rooms had been cleaned, vacuums humming in preparation for Monday's new arrivals, and Edna and Angelo, she in her wheelchair, sat with a snack between them in Angie's office, smiling at each other between bites of a fine Stilton on crackers, washed down with wine from a bottle of good Pinot Grigio. Ned and Bo were in Ned's room, seated across from each other at a table, playing exotic eights. They heard a cackling laugh in the hallway, Natasha of course, and Ned whispered "Oh, God!," and Bo laughed lightly. Ned was sitting very erect in his chair, no longer slumping, which was his usual posture. He felt strong and healthy, and he grinned at Bo, shaking his head.

"Well, she's a bit of nutty fun anyway."

Lisa had left for the airport at 2:00 pm. Ram had driven her there and now sat in his office going over the positions he'd found available in Tallahassee. He'd finished his letter and had begun addressing the envelopes when he heard a knock. It was Melany, his nurse.

"A note for you," her voice muffled by the door between them.

"Okay," Ram said. "Bring it in."

And she did, then left, and Ram opened the envelope and read what was printed there.

> *You are invited to a party in celebration of the ending of the Day of the Dead week. The ballroom at the Sea Burst this evening, eight o'clock pm.*
>
> *Please come.*
>
> *Angelo Camp.*
>
> *P.S: Casual dress if you wish. No bones required.*

Why not, Ram thought. No Lisa. No more work. Nothing to do. Those left at the Sea Burst had received this invitation too, even Natasha and the photographer.

"Are you okay, Charly?" Ernesto said.

A lazy afternoon, and Charly was sitting on a blanket on the beach, toying with his gear, a small chemistry set and the magnets. His mind appeared to be elsewhere, and Ernesto, lounging in a beach chair facing him and the sea beyond, was concerned. Charly looked up at him.

"Yes, I am," he said. "But I'm sad that the week is over. And I'm sad too that Mrs. Hobby broke her foot."

"Well, it isn't actually broken," Ernesto said.

"I know that," Charly said. "But I like the sound of it. She has broken her foot." He laughed lightly. "It's a sprain. Either the calcaneofibular ligament or the posterior talofibular one."

Ernesto laughed. "How in the world did you figure that?"

"At the hotel," Charly answered. "I heard Mr. Camp and Mrs. Hobby talking about it, what doctor Chopra said. Then I looked it up. In *Gray's Anatomy*."

"Where?"

"Over there. At the hotel. They have a lot of books. There's a little library."

"I didn't know that," his father said. He was smiling. He looked happy.

"You look happy," Charly said.

"Well, you know, I guess I am. This has been a good week for me. I liked the work, and I like the place. Some excitement for sure, what with that death down the beach and all. But I'm feeling good."

Charly hesitate before he spoke.

"What about mother?" he finally asked. "Are you still thinking of her?"

"Well, thinking yes. But she's gone, Charly. And I think I can leave her there now. It's been a long time for sure, but now I think it might be changing."

"That's good," Charly said, and he reached out and touched his father on his bare knee.

"Well, here we are, old friends and new, gathered to mark the ending of this week-long celebration. It has been quite a week: a dead body found on the beach; two violent storms within which revelers prevailed, at least in the first case; and the arrival, without precedent, of a herd of sheep. And now, on top of all this, we have a severely sprained ankle.

"But let us not dwell upon these misfortunes. It's been a good week as well, even here in this hotel. People have met and become friends, and in some cases much more. Few animals and humans were injured, none seriously, and a young boy has proven his mettle.

"I had thought to host this occasion in the bar and to ask Mr. Bo Bogardus to entertain us with his music. A foolish idea. This is, after all, a party. No work allowed, only pleasure. There will be music, for talking and dancing, but it will have to come through these speakers behind me. So I hope this small ballroom space will prove adequate for our enjoyments. I welcome you all. And, in a few moments, just as I finish this windy speech, the music will begin, and soon after, the food will be served.

"This is the day, this week, when the dead come alive and ride down from those heavens above, here to spend time with their relatives. For a while at least. We all know that the dead can still be alive, at least in memory. But memory can be a trickster, as when it holds on too long. And we can be its victims, living only, in the most important living, in the past.

"So on this evening of the last Day of the Dead, I want to say goodbye to all the celebrants, even the drunks; goodbye to itinerant vendors, piñatas and costumes; goodbye to those sheep and the various other animals who found their way into town, often bewildered in the company of dancing bones. Goodbye, goodbye. And lastly, and most importantly, I want to say goodbye to the dead, those who have descended in search of that earthly peace, the one that can only be found among relatives, lovers, and friends. They have had their week, now it's time to return to the heavens where they belong."

There was a bar set into the wall at the back of the room, and once the applause had ended and Angie had moved out among his guests, a few went there for drinks. Natasha Burm was among them, escorted by the photographer Ned and Bo had seen at work on the beach. He was a slim, handsome man, dark, probably European, and he must have been five foot nine or ten, yet he looked like a child beside Natasha in her six foot four.

"Andre," she said, looking down at him, "Would you order to me g and t?"

She had her own idea of casual wear. She wore slightly baggy pants above high spiked heels. Though loose in the legs, her attractive behind was tucked in tight. Her top, a manly looking shirt, the tails tied in a knot at the thin line of her bare waist, was made of a flimsy flowered silk, and its drape guarded the shapes of her small breasts, unless she turned her torso slightly, at will. That long hair, gathered into a bun on top of her head, those prominent cheek bones and puffy lips.

"I will go now, Andre, for doing time against others." This said in a somewhat imperious fashion. She left Andre at the bar then and strutted away.

"Here she comes," Bo said. He was standing beside Ned who was standing beside his mother's wheelchair, leaning over and talking with her in a warm, civilized way.

"So now, Mr. Ned. This, then, is your mother to be introdusit to me?"

"Ah, Natasha!" Ned said, having risen up to his full height. He looked up at her. "Yes, this is my mother. Natasha Burm meet Edna Hobby."

Natasha bent way over and took Edna's hand. "Please it to meet you." She spoke very quietly and smiled, and Edna, feeling like some damned invalid in this lousy chair, shook her hand vigorously and smiled back.

Then Natasha rose up and looked over at Bo, then back at Ned. She smiled, a very broad smile indeed.

"Two handsomest young men," she said. "I will it for you to enjoy it together." She reached out and touched Ned on the shoulder. "I had never thought it, Ned, but now is it looked over by me. *Pazdravlyay-oos*! Means it congratulations to where I am coming from." She smiled again and winked, then turned to find her Andre and join with the others.

The police chief was there, as well as the mayor and a few other dignitaries, and Ram Chopra was in conversation with them. Nothing serious, just some jokes about the week's events and some laughter. Ernesto, standing a few inches back from the group, had been listening, though he felt somewhat out of place in the gathering. He moved to the side of the room, took out his phone and called Charly who was up in their room watching the Nature Channel on television. He told him he'd be late and that he should go to bed whenever he felt like it, but not too late. The two would be leaving tomorrow morning. They'd decided on Charly's dinner, sitting side by side on the bed, selecting things from the room service menu, an exciting enterprise. A cheese burger, with french fries, and a large Coke and a chocolate sundae for dessert. He liked them to melt down a little, get softened up. This one could sit there until he'd finished his dinner. Then it would be just right.

"You're okay up there? How's nature?"

"A good show about wild animals, in Africa? You should see this stuff."

"Well, good, and how was dinner?"

"Very good, dad, and now the sundae's ready."

"Great! Enjoy it. And call me if you need anything."

"Okay, I will. Have a good time."

Ram had moved to spend some time with Angie, checking out this tall drink of theatrical water and her escort, or maybe her lover, as he went. Were Lisa here, she'd have a good talk with the photographer. God, he missed her. Maybe he should call her, but then she might not be home yet, flight delays and all. But he could leave a message. Well, maybe he shouldn't push it. He'd call tomorrow.

"Who is that incredibly tall woman?"

"Here for a photoshoot, swimming suits and beach wear down in the surf. They've checked in for three days. I believe Ned Hobby knows her, but I don't know what that might be about."

"Well, she's really something," Ram said.

"That she is," said Angie.

The music was dreamy, both vocal and instrumental, quiet jazz tunes. Bo was listening intermittently, but all the rest were drifting their friendly conversations over it as counterpoint. *You Go to My Head, At Last, More Than You Know.* Natasha and Andre took the floor, and Bo and Ned joined them. Neither had danced with a man before, and though initially shy as to who should lead, they quickly worked their way into a groove, not cheek to cheek, only their hands touching hands, shoulders and backs. Natasha swirled by them, Andre trying hard to keep up, and others in the room watched them, especially Edna Hobby, leaning out to the side of her chair the better to see. Soon the scent of food drifted into the room, followed by a long table on wheels that was pushed in by a young woman server and the chief himself, in his tall, floppy hat. All heads turned in anticipation, even those of the dancers.

First came the plates, silver and cloth napkins, followed by a large tureen containing Beef Bourguignon, its rich scent apparent when the tureen top was removed. Then there were serving bowls, roasted potatoes, asparagus, pearl onions, and a large dish of baby spinach, to be fried by the chef himself, to order, on a hot plate halfway down the table. Then came cheeses, Stilton, St. Andre, and an aged Wisconsin Cheddar, a bowl of small lightly toasted bread at the ready. And at the tables end, dessert, baked Alaska and cherries jubilee. Wine, and at the meal's end, liqueurs, could be had at the bar at the back of the room. The dancing stopped, though the music continued, and all moved to the tables. Angie was first, and he arranged a plate for Edna, the food displayed in an attractive manner for her pleasure. Then Angie, plateless himself, moved around the room, the perfect host, passing a few words with everyone.

After they had all eaten their fill, conversation and dancing resumed, and as the clock moved toward conclusion, most of the dignitaries took their leave and in a while even the police chief and the mayor and Natasha and Andre left, and only the principle invitees remained, those six who had spent their week at the Sea Burst, minus Lisa and Charly. They spoke of the week's events, the storms, the costumes, the riotous and subdued behaviors. And each spoke of the future, some tentatively, others with certainty. Ernesto had little to say. He would go back home, to work and to care for his children. Charly had called to say he was going to bed. No need for his father to check on him anymore. "Good night, Dad," he'd said. "Have a good time."

His dad reached into his pocket and felt for his cigarette case, a sleek old silver thing, an inheritance, that held only a half dozen. He allowed himself three a day, and on some days he smoked nothing. He went to the door leading to the boardwalk and beach, while behind him the party continued, though the tone was now low and very casual, nothing much else to say, but for a few words in preparation for parting. He stepped out into the night, onto the boardwalk. There was a full moon in the sky out over the sea, and after he'd lit up, he just stood there, enjoying the darkness, the moon, and the calm ocean.

Chapter 19

APHRODITE, 10:15 pm

I have given them their lives, and now they are on their own. Most are healthy and possibly in love, the past finally behind them, or at least headed there, gone with the celebrated dead into appropriate oblivion. All but for Ernesto and of course Charly, who sits watching the nature channel. Or perhaps he is now sleeping, alone, singular, and brilliant.

I have walked to the mountain and have seen, in moonlight, the shepherd and his flock bedded down in a tight cluster high on the ski trail. I heard the bleating. Then I walked to the beach, where I heard only the sea lapping at the sand near my feet as I made my way, in a glorious night, back to the boardwalk and toward the town.

I will no longer think of my father, nor the part I played in his demise. The police will no doubt find me, my full name etched into that first metal profile on his charm bracelet. I will have no story to tell them, though they may find my letter among his belongings, here at the Sea Burst. All I know is that he is no longer behind me, urging me on, and I believe that soon I can stop walking. Maybe I can do it even now.

Yes, glorious, the moonlight forming a crystal river on the sea reaching from the beach to the dark horizon, a warm breeze fingering my short hair. I have taken my cap off, unloaded the empty soda bottles from my knapsack, unbuttoned the light jacket I always wear when walking in summer. The weight I carry is lighter now. I feel a spring in my step.

Coming abreast of the curve of the ballroom, those tall windows, I step from the boardwalk and move close to them. I can see into where the few remaining celebrants stand in a loose circle, talking, smiling at each other. There's Angelo, standing beside Edna in her wheelchair, his hand on her shoulder. And there are Ned and Bo, animated, smiling. They both look elegant in their fine, casual garments. Ned shifts lightly on his feet. He may no longer be in pain. Bo is speaking to Ram, who stands across from them, his eyes a bit unfocused. He's no doubt thinking of Lisa, who is by this time back in Florida, probably thinking of him. All arms move in abbreviated gestures, their heads tilt to the side, their torsos, at times, lean forward while making a point. But from the waist down they are relaxed, stationary, at ease. They seem to have nowhere to go, not now. They are where they are.

Then a man disengages from the group. He crosses the room and goes to the door facing the beach. I see him come out and move to the boardwalk. He lights a cigarette, faces the sea.

"Ernesto," I call out softly, then see his head turn in my direction.

"Yes?" he says, and I move from the windows to the boardwalk and approach him. He is tall, and I am small beside him.

"Ernesto," I say, looking up into his dark eyes.

"You know me," he says.

"Yes, I do," I say. "I'm Ann Brown. Let's walk down to the water and sit for a while on the sand. What do you say?"

He says nothing, but I drop the weight of my backpack, and he takes my hand, and we move to a place a few feet back from the surf line and sit down beside each other, very close, but not touching.

We speak of things in our lives then, just those details that make life real. He tells me about his son and daughter, his work with animals, Mrs. Frank, who cares for his children while he's at work, the nature of his house in Watertown. I tell him about college, cross country running, my mother's long illness, where I was born and come from.

Then, after a while, we are silent, feeling the presence of each other, watching the moon's crystal trail on the water, and near the moon, the blink of the north star. The red and green lights of a solitary fishing boat, way out in the dis-

tance, move lazily across the horizon. A flock of night birds drift over the moon's face. They seem close enough to land.

He is not like those men I have slept with over the years, and what I desire, sitting in the sand beside him, is not sex or romance, but the comfort of being in one place, with another, and staying there.

A light cool breeze comes in from the north, and I shiver.

"Are you cold?" he asks, and before I can deny it, he puts his arm around me and holds me close. There is nothing seductive in this gesture, just concern for my well being. I imagine myself as a small animal under his care.

"Thank you," I say.

Then the lights in the ballroom behind us are extinguished, and the moon seems to grow larger, the stars brighter. He is there, holding me close, and all of a sudden a decent life seems possible, even likely. I can see it as if it were already written down in our future, and I think he can see it too.

Toby Olson on *Walking*—

It's an old story with writers, when they speak of character, that at some point in the writing the characters they've invented seem to come alive, and I decided to write a book in which the characters actually *do* come alive.

My writer (really, she's a story teller) is Aphrodite, a woman in her 30s who can't stop walking. She speaks directly to us, and as she moves along, she creates characters before our eyes. But then something happens, and these characters step away from her, move beyond her control, take on a life of their own. Much more could be said about this, but I won't say it. You can read the book. I could have explained everything and made it a beach novel, but that's not the book I wanted to write. This is just that—every word and comma is the way I want it.

And there's more. There's profound loss; there's a serial killer—not incidentally, Aphrodite's father—;

there's a Day of the Dead celebration; there's a brilliant child. And there's also a love story. Characters
leave their tortured minds behind and find redemp-
tion in love.

I attempted to present this love as a light parody of
a romance novel, and many loves there are.

There are two books that precede *Walking* when it
comes to this business with character, and they both
inspired my attempts in this book. They are *At-Swim-
Two-Birds*, by Flann O'Brien (pseudonym of Brian
O'Nolan) and *Mulligan Stew*, by Gilbert Sorrentino.
Even in their absence, I thank them.